Prose and Con

Poems Against the Brexit Machine

By

Major Rager

First published in Great Britain in 2017

Illustrations by Madeleina Kay

Designed by NL

A CIP catalogue record for this book is available from the British Library

ISBN 9781973316404

Contents

Foreword

You know that only the rich will benefit from the coming Brexit disaster machine – the newspaper owners, the politicians on the make, the shadowy billionaires who funded the lies and deceit. You know that the rest of us will suffer the poverty and irrelevance of the inevitable decline of Britain. It's already started. Will of the people, our arses. Only 37 per cent of the British electorate voted for a Brexit suicide. And many of those have realised that they were conned.

So follow your instincts. Gird your lions, armour your buttocks, polish your Brexitplates for the fightback against the Brexit scourge. Bugger Boris, jettison Jacob, f—k Farage and Field. Battle the Brexit darkness. Be a true patriot in the best interests of your country. Buying this book full of witty, fascinating poetic truths is your first step.

It's aimed at intelligent people, those prepared to examine their opinions on the anvil of evidence. We can't promise any unicorns, or even sunlit uplands, but we do promise release from the self-interested crap of politicians and newspaper owners.

Introduction

Brexit was fuelled by a heady cocktail of naked populism, lies, and a large wad of dirty cash. Brexit will be ended by a more thoughtful version of popular activism. Our Huguenot poster-boy for Brexit and Trump, Nigel Farage, told us to vote with our hearts. This was code for 'Don't think', and we fell for it. Now the people have thought about it for nearly eighteen months and our heads are telling us, 'Don't do this.'

Moreover, our government still cannot explain the motive for the Brexit crime. They cannot tell us which version of Brexit we are aiming for – clean, dirty, black, blue, retro, trance etc. – nor point to any significant benefits of leaving the EU. Indeed, it has become plain that Brexit offers us a bleak future of privatised health and social care; unprotected employment conditions; a servile economy of low wages; environmental rape; and a Brexodus of major industries from the UK.

However, as any marketer will tell you, our hearts rule our heads, especially when we have already made a decision and may look silly if we are seen to change our minds. So, we are currently trapped with our politicians on nearly all sides like the proverbial frog in a pan, which fails to register the gradual increase in temperature until it is boiled to death. I believe that it is always a mistake to remain silent when what you are doing is fundamentally wrong. However, many people do not believe they now have the right to right the wrong that was Brexit. These include fatigued Remain voters and Leavers in quiet regret. How then do we unlock the paralysis that has gripped our parliamentary decision makers? Well, there are no magic bullets and we need a veritable tsunami of initiatives in the absence of a coherent Remain movement. The poets and writers in this book are making their own small contribution to the cause via 'prose and cons'.

I said to my wife on 25 June 2016: 'This is not like an election, where three days afterwards we'll forget about it. This will run and run and run.' It has done. For the first time in my history, I was moved to take to the streets in my 'rage against the Brexit machine', initially through performing songs at the No. 10 Vigil and eventually through a project called Rage Against the Brexit Machine: www.brexitrage.com. I am an unusual blend of business academic, author, business consultant, scientist and musician, and used these skills to write and produce a stream of satirical songs. Our songs included the swamp-blues track 'No, Jeremy Corbyn', the eighteenth-century Tory trance floor groove 'Jacob Rees-Moog' and a song written especially for Dorset for Europe to support their dream of a movement of people in underwear called 'Pants to Brexit'. Sadly, their movement turned out to be nothing more than a bowel movement. But it did produce the idea for this book, which brings poetry, song lyrics and prose together in one place.

Our writers came from far and wide – all over the UK and beyond – united not by dogma or politics but with one vision, to Break Brexit Before Brexit Breaks Britain. Some write poems, some songs, others prose, but all are committed to ending the Brexit nightmare.

Some of the pieces are ever so slightly edgy, reflecting unresolved feelings of rage due to our government's decision to treat 27 per cent of the population as a strong majority. This will continue until Brexit is laid to rest.

Brexit is itself a symptom of a much greater set of socio-economic issues that we must face in the fourth industrial revolution. Sweeping such issues under the carpet will not make them go away. We seek a better Britain in a united Europe – that's hardly a sonnet, but you get the general idea. Poetry alone won't stop Brexit: it is something like a hydra, which grows new heads when attacked, shape-shifting to avoid a fixed position. We hope that our contribution weakens the monster in some small way, while doing some good for our chosen basket of charities: Teenage Cancer Trust, the Stroke Association, the Trussell Trust, Save the Children, the Donkey Sanctuary, Cats Protection League, Oxfam, Guide Dogs for the Blind, ColaLife, Sane, Rainbow Trust and Water Aid.

Peter Cook

Poems

Talking with the taxman about poetry

In this section we find poetry that bites. Yes, these are not love lines or odes to joy, but sad, funny and satirical pieces that tell stories of hopelessness, powerlessness, inhumanity, duplicity, levity and so on. They ride the emotional rollercoaster of Brexit. Enjoy the big Brexit dipper and the vice of treason.

If poetry was allowed in the UK gutter press and more than three words considered acceptable as a headline, I would have summed this section of the book up as Brexit Bards Bite Brexit Before Brexit Bites Britain's Bottomline! In this context we have a series of witty limericks and short poems plus a series of longer pieces, which discuss all aspects of Brexit. Read them with understanding and with a determination to stand up for the future of your country as an open-minded, outward-looking, tolerant European nation that rejects the isolation and disaster of Brexit.

The will of the people was informed by the will o' the wisp, in other words wilful lies. Brexit has since become the ill of the people. Some of us are very sick indeed. One of my friends even ended it all just recently and undoubtedly the aftermath of the Brexit referendum will have been one of the factors that contributed to his sad decision.

Prose and Cons – Poems Against The Brexit Machine

Sick of lies
Sick of denial
Sick of 57 varieties of Brexit
Sick of EU citizens being treated as bargaining chips
Sick of incompetent MPs
Sick of self-harm
Sick of the Dunning-Kruger effect
Sick of being sick

Peter Cook

The Stubborn Brexiteer

There was a stupid Brexiteer
Who couldn't change his mind.
Even though he knew we're screwed,
He stayed for ever blind.
His money became worthless,
His job went overseas,
But still he couldn't say he's wrong
With Britain on its knees.

Come the day of reckoning,
He just explained it all
By blaming all them foreigners
For Britain's rapid fall.
And even on his deathbed,
As he drank his final cup,
He couldn't see that Britons
Had really fucked it up.

Alas for stubborn Brexiteers
Who wave their flags so fast,
And call themselves true patriots
Because of Britain's past.
They condemned us all to poverty;
They never had a doubt,
Because they read the tabloid press
And couldn't work it out.

Another type of Brexiteer
Has bank accounts offshore.
He's a multimillionaire
Who sees a chance of more.
The EU says that he must pay,
Like others do, his tax.
And so he funds the Brexit cause
To doctor all the facts.

NL

The Lord's Brexit Prayer

Our Mother (Theresa)
Who art in Whitehall,
Shallow be thy name.

Thy (disUnited) Kingdom come,
EU will be done,
In court as it is in Brexit.

(For)give us this day our *Daily Mail*,
And forGove us our sins,
As we forGove those (bastards
Farage, Davis, Fox, Leadsom)
Who have sinned against us.

And lead us not into Trumptation,
But deliver us from Boris.

For thine is the treason,
Thy tower and the Tory,
For ever and ever.
EU.

Peter Cook

Brexit or Bust

The country's an inferno:
The core has reached the crust,
The gable end is gaping.
It's Brexit, then, or bust.

The sensation is seismic.
The sky is filled with dust.
The corporation's cracking.
It's Brexit, then, or bust.

They're manning their mansions,
Preparing for the day
When *everything* is privatised.
It's free trade all the way.

Hauling up the drawbridges,
Filling up their moats,
Battening down the hatches,
Rebottoming their boats.

Blowing up the bridges,
An offshore we've become,
A haven for the craven,
All types of tawdry scum.

While seeds of revolution
Are blown into the air,
Particles on pavements,
Explosions everywhere.

The country's an inferno:
The roofs are red with rust.
Babylon is burning.
It's Brexit, then, or bust.

A mother-ship catastrophe,
To watch it is a must.
It's mayhem in the making.
It's Brexit, then, or bust.

Robert Cunliffe

A Dog's Brexit

The Trump asked
The May, and
The May asked
The Brexit SPAD:
'Could we have Covfefe for
The soiled heist of Brexit?'
The May asked the Brexit SPAD
To ask the new
Home Secretary:
'I'll go and tell the cow
Now,
Although her dad's just dead.'

The Brexit SPAD,
She curtsied,
And went and told
Home Secretary:
'Don't forget Covfefe for
The soiled heist of Brexit.'
Home Secretary
Said sleepily,
'You'd better tell
Their Majesties
That many people nowadays
Drop Climate Change
Instead.'

The Brexit SPAD
Said, 'Frack me!'
And went to

Major Rager   Page 14

Her May-jesty.
She curtsied to the Maybot, and
Put U-turns in her head:
'Excuse me,
Your May-jesty,
For taking of
The liberty,
But Fracking is achievable,
If very thinly
Spread.'

The May said,
'Oh!'
And went to
His Trumpesty:
'Talking about climate deals
And soiled heists of Brexit:
Many people
Now think that
Fracking is
Quite profitable.
Would you like UK to drop
The climate treaties dead?'

The Trump said,
'Rather!'
And then he said,
'Yes, come with me!'
And dropped the treaty dead.
'Nobody,'
He whimpered,
'Could call me

A pussy man;
I only want
Covfefe
And a wall,
And all the bread.'

The May held
His little hand,
And went to
The Brexit SPAD.
The Brexit SPAD
Said, 'There, there!'
And went to see Rudd.
The cow said,
'There, there!
We're only "disappointed";
Take the NHS, and fracking,
And a Brexit deal instead.'

The May took
The Covfefe
And brought it to
His Trumpesty;
The Trump said,
'Covfefe?'
And bounced out of bed.
'Nobody,' he said,
As he frisked her
Tenderly,
'Nobody,' he said,
As he slid down the poll ratings,
'No one

Major Rager   Page 16

In the Senate
Will dare to impeach me,
But
I DO want oil and coal and climate
Treaties dead.'

Jane Berry

Have You Taken Leave of Your Senses?

Some people have
Taken Leave of their senses.
But we Remainers
Are saner.

Have you taken Leave
Of your senses?
Don't worry; come back
And stay on track.

We are forgiving,
So rejoin the living.
Don't take the ride
Of cliff-edge suicide.

Vicki Harris

Brexit Is a Mess

Save us all, they're breaking Britain,
But our future's not yet written.
Stop these lying politicians.
The bus sold lies; their own admission.

You've a limited warning for Remain intervention.
When the EU flags are flying, prepare for redemption.

We must stop them all:
Stop them blinding you with politics,
And stuffing up their policies,
Cos Brexit means apocalypse.

Don't let that rampant Maybot tell you lies,
No, no, no, no, no.
She'll use your vote to leave to bleed you dry.

It's like a dagger to the heart.
Brexit is a mess, Brexit is a mess, oh yes, oh yes, Brexit is
a mess.

Before Britain leaves,
And our country sinks,
Our food gets crap and sterling sinks,
When the welfare state
leaves you in the cold,
And there's euthanasia for the old:

Major Rager   Page 19

You've a limited warning for Remain intervention,
And the Brexit plans will crumble: we'll stop their
corruption.
As Europe looks on,
To keep our credibility,
We're staying European now:
To function it's necessary.
Only choosing to remain can save us now.
No, no, no, no, no:
Brexit's a nightmare that we won't allow.

It's like a dagger to the heart.
Brexit is a mess, Brexit is a mess, oh yes, oh yes, Brexit is
a mess.

Annie Bell

Five Haiku

Nigel, we noticed:
Mantra to manic, exposed:
Ram at it, conman.

A meeting of minds
lacking true diplomacy
it wasn't Priti

Boris, through wheat fields
'I ran' ruined your chances.
True ladykiller?

Davis, find, from your
Critical thinking gap, a
Cathartic inkling.

Re-smack down the poor.
Re-smog cities, Re-smug rich.
Vote Jacob Fleece-Mob.

Jane Berry

Lines Composed upon the First Anniversary of
Independence Day, 24 June 2017

A year ago today,
The People had their say.
Our leader, pace Faust,
Made a pact, his foes to oust:
From UKIP he would win
The support to vote him in!
Putting party above nation
(To insufficient indignation),
He won!
But he'd staked our Now and Then
For the keys to Number 10.

For contingent on the plan
Of this glib and shallow man
Was that vote a year ago:
To the polls he had us go.
But he hadn't banked on lies,
And to his great surprise,
He found he'd up it mucked –
So now the country's fucked.
He lost!
He'd put his party first,
But we all came off the worst.

The new PM, named May,
Is no better, I must say.
And for blatant party gain
She would have us vote again.
The instructions on the toolkit

Said she couldn't do but walk it;
But the nation proved more able:
Now she's crumbs beneath the table.
She lost!*
She put her party first
And now *she*'s come off worst.

How do we stand today?
A nation on its way?
No.
Divided, sick and bitter,
In obeisance to the Quitter;
Where the nasty hold the whip
As the seams of Britain rip.
And our sloth, complacent past
Catches up with us at last.
More sovereignty? God forbid:
Look how we used it when we did!
We've ALL lost.
This imagined island rock?
An international laughing stock.

*Come on – she DID!

Peter Roberts

The Crumblies
with apologies to Edward Lear

They went to sea in a sieve, they did,
In a sieve they went to sea:
In spite of all their friends could say,
On a winter's morn, on a stormy day,
In a sieve they went to sea!

And when the sieve spun round and round,
And everyone cried, 'You'll all be drowned!'
They called aloud, 'So our sieve ain't a duck –
But we don't give a button! We don't give a fuck!
In a sieve we're off to sea!'

Far and few, far and few
Are the lands where the Quitters live.
Their brains are small, and their tongues are blue,
And they went to sea in a sieve.

They sailed away in a sieve, they did;
But that sieve, it sailed so slow,
With only a beautiful Union Jack
Tied upside-down with their cack-handed knack,
And so small that their sieve wouldn't go.
And every one said, who saw the winds blow,
'Oh won't they soon be upset, you know!
For the sky is so dark and that sieve is a slum,
And happen what may, it's so blatantly dumb
In a sieve to sail so slow!'

Far and few, far and few
Are the lands where the Quitters live.
Their brains are small, and their tongues are blue,
And they went to sea in a sieve.

The water it soon came in, it did,
The water it soon came in;
So to keep them dry they wrapped their feet
In the *Daily Mail* all folded neat,
And they fastened it down with a pin.
And they passed each night more and more on the piss,
And each of them screamed, 'Who'll we blame now for
this?
Though the sky be dark and the voyage be long,
Yet we never can think we were rash or wrong,
So it must be the Muslims or … er … um … er …
Yes: the Swiss!'

Far and few, far and few
Are the lands where the Quitters live.
Their brains are small and their tongues are blue,
And they went to sea in a sieve.

And all night long they sailed away;
And when the sun went down,
They drunkenly warbled a lunatic's song
To the echoing sound of a funeral gong,
And not once their spirits did frown!
'Oh Jacob Rees-Mogg! How happy we are,
That we live in a sieve and we are what we are!
While all night long under moonlight pale,
We sink away with a flag for a sail,

In the stench of our effluent brown!'

Far and few, far and few
Are the lands where the Quitters live.
Their brains are small, and their hands are blue,
And they went to sea in a sieve.

They sailed o'er the Western Sea, they did,
For the land where the money tree grows.
But they took with them nowt but a horse and a cart,
And many such things (as much use as a fart),
And they gained but a dribbling nose.
For they'd mortgaged their house, and they'd sold their in-laws,
And they'd shared their stale memories of football and wars
Over forty sad bottles of what came to hand,
And a packet of Doritos.

Far and few, far and few
Are the lands where the Quitters live.
Their brains are small and their tongues are blue,
And they went to sea in a sieve.

But in twenty years they all came back,
In twenty years or more,
And everyone said, 'How small they've grown!
For they've been to the States, and the Horrible Zone,
And they've seen the American maw!'
But they drank to their health, and gave them a feast
Of mussels from Brussels and fruits from the east;
And everyone said, 'Now as long as we live,

We never will go off to sea in a sieve –
But dance by its waves ever more!'

Oh far and few, far and few
Are the lands where the Quitters lived;
For their brains were so small that their tongues fell out,
And they sold
Their souls
For a sieve.

Peter Roberts

What Has Brexit Done for Us?

What has Brexit done for us?
Corrupt politicians; lies on a bus;
Pound's value dropping, no sign of stopping
Any time soon.

What has Brexit done for us?
Hate and division; lack of vision;
Brainwashed by the papers; political capers;
Corruption and gloom.

What has Brexit done for us?
EU ties unravel; loss of free travel;
Rascists are legion; poor people needin';
No one to stop 'them v. us'.

What has Brexit done for us?
Mucked up our country,
That's what!

Lesley Bell

A New Day

Paint the White House black,
Tear down Big Ben:
Our lives have been hijacked
By the angry white men.

Cry, 'Open the gate
To the floodgates of gall!'
Cry, 'Let in the hate
And build up that wall!'

They make our countries
As a truth-free zone,
And hate by degrees
Freezes through to the bone.

Open your arms in the dark,
My fellow men:
Let your love make an ark,
Let light shine again.

For, deep in the night
Where the nightmares are born,
Comes the glimmer of light
That heralds the dawn.

Bow down to your sorrows
To pick up the plough:
Let seeds of love grow
That we start to plant now.

Major Rager

Raise your voices, shout 'Yes'
Where they would shout 'No,'
And with hope light the furnace,
And strengthen the glow.

There will rise a new day
Out of the deepest night;
And the House that was grey
Will once more be White.

The bells that were broken
Will be forged whole again;
And who hears their call
Will answer with all.

Gemma Knowles

Tea Leavers

If I ask you,
'Do you want some tea?'
And you say
Yes,
I can serve you
Any amount
At any temperature
In any kind of container,
Of

Mint tea, matcha tea,
Herbal tea, horrible tea,
Black tea, green tea,
White tea, fruit tea,
Beef tea, coca tea,
Chai tea, calamitea,
Rooibos tea, rosehip tea,
Iced tea, insanitea ...
The list is endless.

I can serve it
With no lumps,
One lump, two lumps,
Ten lumps, fifty lumps,
Infinity lumps
Or heffalumps;
No milk,
Cow's milk, cat's milk,
Goat's milk, stoat's milk,
Coconut milk

Or Castlemilk.

There might be
Whisky in it, rum in it,
Huskies or my thumb in it –
And you can never claim
It isn't what you asked for.

'But I wanted English breakfast!'
You'd wail about your fate.
'Oh, you never said,' I'd say,
'And now it's just too late.'

So here's the moral of my tale,
The lesson of my fable:
Never just say yes, unless
You know what's on the table.

Paul Brown

A Victory for Common Sense

We are the demented offspring
Of 1960s rock legends,
Soft and mollycoddled.
And we need Brexit,
Or something like it,
To put that right.

A return to core values,
A renewed Pax Britannica,
Where, no matter what happens,
Or how much it hurts,
It happens out of sight.

We need our backbone back,
Our stiff upper lip,
And the rod of iron
That bends to form
The grin that bears it.

We need to shred the rulebook,
The checks and balances.
Justice is against us.
We need to cry more,
In fear.

Robert Cunliffe

Ode to Brexit

Our government's committed, Brexitshitters just
the same.
Is committed like committable?
Are we all insane?
'So bring it on!' you hear us cry:
We're ready for you; do or die!
Brexit, we're not scared of you;
We thought we'd make Brexshitter stew!

We know we're great, next all we need's
Remainers now to take the lead,
And show the world, who stand and stare,
That Europhiles are well prepared.
With 'Bollocks to Brexit' battlecry,
We'll fight for Britain, do or die!

We'll teach them not to mess with us,
Though we fight fair, they won't beat us.
So is all this a bit gung-ho?
Some might say yes, some might say no.
We're so damn good, you Brexshit toads,
We've even time to pen this ode!
So spare a thought for plenty who
Are fighting Brexit till Brexit's through.

Lesley Bell

At the Bar of the Rule Britannia

You seen them Europeans?
Take our dosh, just like a thief, yeah?
They make the rules, they take our jobs—
What you lookin' at me fer?
May doesn't follow footie cos she
Finks it's all beneaf er.
But if she did she'd understand:
The EU's just like FIFA.

We started the internationals –
1872 or 3, yeah?
The Football 'sociation:
That was England was the leader.
The Europeans stole it then;
They 'ad to be the chief, yeah.
I done all my research, see,
And the EU's just like FIFA.

It were all them Europeans:
Set it up to give us grief, yeah.
They tricked us into joining
All along, so that's my beef, yeah.
It's all a con to do us down,
Set up by Edward Heef, yeah.
And that's my point I'm makin':
See, the EU's just like FIFA.

After the war, we walked away;
That's World War One, y'see. Fer
Several years then we were out.

We missed our chance to be fer
Once, fer all, right out in front.
I ask you now: What's V fer?
We shoulda made our own rules then.
The EU's just like FIFA.

I read about it in the *Sun*:
That whistle-blowing geezer.
It were them oo let Qataris in,
That immigrant lot – see fer
What it's worth, they're all the same.
I just can't make it briefer.
You 'eard what Andy Burnham said:
The EU's just like FIFA.

I seen that *Panorama* fing:
It's just a bleedin' free-fer-
All – Bungs and tax and rip-offs.
And the Russian fing goes deeper;
That's 'ow they stole 2018.
So it' just a big relief
We'll only play UK teams now.
The EU's just like FIFA.

Jane Berry

True Patriots

True patriots do what will make Britain great:
They don't wave flags, shout slogans or dictate,
Don't heed propaganda from government or press:
They recognise why Britain is in such a mess.

They read the signs of an impending threat
That will see the economy sink into debt.
They note British companies seeking a base
In Europe where there's a large marketplace.

They see the health service in deep neglect
For lack of staff due to Brexit's effect.
The poor, the sick, the jobless who suffer
Will find that their lives will get much tougher.

They know that Brexit's foundations are fake,
Funded by rich billionaires on the take.
They know that more people now recognise
That they have been fooled by elaborate lies.

So how can true patriots dispel the hatred,
To heal the self-harm that Brexit's created,
To counter the suicide Britain is courting,
And the mistrust that the media's exhorting?

They listen to experts who've studied the facts
Based on evidence of the likely impacts,
And use their intelligence to find the right key
To ensure their future prosperity.

Major Rager

They see we will sink if we live in the past,
So they widen horizons for a future that lasts.
Patriots rebuild a true Europe of nations,
For there's nothing to gain from bleak isolation.

Brexit is toxic, of that there's no doubt:
Britain's sole chance is to turn it about.
True patriots will lobby to put all that right,
And overturn Brexit's paranoid flight.

So true patriots of Britain, rise up, take your place,
Don't tarnish your country in the Brexit disgrace.
The empire's long gone, its flag is now furled,
So work with your partners to build a new world.

A world that looks outward to new innovations
That meet the real challenges facing all nations.
The vision that keeps our planet intact
True patriots will foster the wisdom to act.

NL

Brexit Sonnet 18

with apologies to Bill Shakespeare

Shall I compare thee to a flight delay?
Boris, Davis, Dr Fox and his mate.
Rough times do shake the darling shoes of May,
And Brexit deals hath all too short a date.

Sometimes too hot the eye of reason shines,
But oft is its significance obscured.
They say that Remainers have nothing but
whines
And that a Brexit summer is assured.

Trade deals yet to be confirmed o'er the seas
Will keep possession of our privilege.
They need us more than we need them, thou sees,
But you may not afford a German fridge.

So long as men can breathe and eyes can see,
So long lives hope ... and maybe sanity.

Keith Glazzard

Will of the People

Would you ask a baker to repair your old car,
Or a mechanic to thread out a difficult suture,
Or a blind man to look at a faraway star,
Or a brickie to forecast your country's future?

So why on earth did we ask those who don't know
To make decisions on large complex matters?
Like how national economies can better grow
And not leave the country's finances in tatters.

Real challenging topics like our global trade,
How manufacturing markets gestate,
How international agreements are made,
And how Britain's wealth and its jobs integrate.

How inward investment can be better created
To nourish the growth of a progressive nation;
And the interconnections that must be related
To avoid the terrible scourge of inflation.

So off we all went to vote on these issues,
Armed with flawed skillsets, at best naïve,
Just propaganda from a prejudiced media
And political chancers all voting for Leave.

So 'the will of the people's' a political war-cry
When 37 per cent of the Brit population
Voted for suicide and ditched its best ally
For keeping the peace and enriching the nation.

Major Rager   Page 40

Into the vacuum leap the big corporations,
Ready to destroy the Brit way of life.
This isn't democracy – it's manipulation!
It leads to destruction and misery and strife.

This tale has a moral for intelligent Brits:
Referendums should be confined to Mars.
No wonder that Britain will be in the shit.
Will of the people, my beautiful arse!

NL

Mighty Blighty

Mighty Blighty,
Plucky, sprightly,
Defender of the real,

Goes abroad
With wooden sword,
And always seals the deal.

Tommy Gun.
We're number one.
We were, are, always will be.

Those Brussels boys
Won't see our ploys:
They'll sign our free-trade treaty.

Bully beef,
With no front teeth,
It's all ours for the taking;

While bureaucrats
Put on their acts,
We'll bring home the bacon.

Heroic, stoic,
Have a go-ic,
We are a one-off nation;

Every night I
Just thank God
That we are not Croatian.

Major Rager

Mighty Blighty,
Lord almighty,
Oh, what doughty foes!

We'll batter them
On beaches,
Come hail, rain, wind or snow!

Afghanistan,
Iran, Japan,
Whatever sticky wicket,

We'll see off
Johnny Foreigner.
We are the winning ticket.

Hand on heart,
Heart on sleeve,
No need here for a breather:

We're fighting fit.
We take no shit.
We take no prisoners either.

In towns, in tents,
In Bruges or Ghent,
Wherever we may be,

Battalions of
Our stallions
Will breeze to victory.

Robert Cunliffe

A Letter to a Brexiter

Dear Brexiter,
Why?
Why do you take my country from me?
Why do you feel the need to be
Flowing with vitriol, spite and hate,
Breaking EUnion with slim mandate?

Dear Brexiter,
Why?
Why do you have to force us apart
From the EU so close to our hearts?
We are left bereft, grieving its loss;
You there, smirking, not giving a toss.

Dear Brexiter,
Why?
Why did you cheat to win the poll
With nasty lies, taking the role
Of fraudulent bullies, breaking away,
When you forced us to swear to fight back that day?

Dear Brexiter,
Why?
Why did you find it so damn hard
To give an inch, when you'd taken a yard?
To embrace the close links to Europe we have,
Instead of which you've left us so sad.

Dear Brexiter,

Major Rager

Why?
Why do you believe the Tory lies
Of Theresa May and her Brexit allies?
Not strong nor stable but she won;
The black widow spider, whose web was spun.

Dear Brexiter,
Why?
Was it really so hard to share?
Couldn't you see that our lives could be there,
With a huge EU family; happy, united?
But you forced the rift and our bond was blighted.

Dear Brexiter,
Why?
Why do you taunt us with inane quips
When questions loom about Brexit?
No answers, then, you lousy quitters?
It's no wonder we named you all Brexshitters.

Dear Brexiter,
Why?
To hell with the consequence; to hell with kin;
You want a divorce? It's really a sin,
To listen to only a fraction of those
Who voted to leave European repose.

Dear Brexiter,
Why?
Why do you let xenophobia and race
Cloud your judgement, making you hate?
We're all European after all:

Major Rager   Page 45

United we stand, divided we fall.

Dear Brexiter,
Why?
As our country unravels, with no more free travel;
Closed borders decreed; no more healthcare that's free.
Are you happy now you've 'got your country back',
Now the pound's gone to shit and our economy's
cracked?

Dear Brexiter,
Why?
Why did you believe the gutter press spin
That's helped get us into the mess that we're in?
Couldn't you tell; couldn't you see
That they lied to your face, yet you still won't trust me?

Dear Brexiter,
Why?
Why scared that migrants steal food off your plate?
They work hard and pay taxes, not ponce off the state.
Look at the facts; find out the truth.
Think of the future you've made for our youth!

Lesley Bell

Young Betrayal

Do you think older Brits give a tuppenny shit
About the world of twenty-thirty-three?
But we'll still be alive
And hoping to thrive
With our friends in a Europe that's free.

Do you think older Brits give a threepenny bit
For the young with a much wider vision?
They vented their spleen
And demolished the dream
Of achieving our chosen ambition.

Do you think older Brits have fourpence of wit
To note empire's flag is now furled?
The blind patriot's cause
To return to what was
When Britain ruled half of the world.

Are the aged so blind they can't open their mind
To a vision of cooperation?
Alas, it's too late,
When the old terminate
The hopes of the young generation.

Don't you think older Brits have proved they're
unfit
By letting intolerance hold sway?
Lies, discontentment
And tabloid resentment
Have taken our future away.

NL

Thinking Democracy

A true democracy would be one that embraced
The values of a true thinking nation
One whose people could think issues through
And make a well-reasoned evaluation.

Making decisions based on good evidence
Is at the root of a strong, mature state,
Where people weigh up all the elements
And subject them to rational debate.

These are the signs of a thinking democracy:
Voters discussing with good-natured grace.
Even though strong opinions may differ,
Respect is habitual in every case.

Contrast all this with the Brexit disaster,
Where raw propaganda ruled the debate:
No thoughtful processing of relevant data,
Just raucous outpourings of mutual hate.

Britons excluded for living in Europe,
And younger people whose land this will be.
Rich billionaires controlling the media
And lie upon lie that no one would see.

No thinking democracy would stand such behaviour!
That's not democracy, it's an outrageous joke.
If we weren't prisoners of misguided zealots
The whole bloody shambles would now be revoked.

Democracy is a most noble concept
That absorbs minorities into its sphere,
That treats every person with equal respect,
And gives them the right to live without fear.

Democracy in Britain has no such ideals.
It's misinformation by the powerful and strong.
While shaped by a media with very few scruples,
A thinking democracy will always be wrong.

The result for the country will be untrammelled misery.
Jobs and safe markets will fast disappear.
When Brexit's flawed chickens come home to roost
The young of Britain will shed many a tear.

NL

Major Rager

We Are ...

We are the liberal elite,
So named because you named us:
The label used to defame us.
We are the liberal elite,
Never stood on our own two feet.
We tried at school and found our way
While you indulged in play,
Or never found the way through:
Shakespeare was too much for you.
The school of hard knocks and – for your strife –
The university of life
Made you who you are today;
Not like those liberals who never pay.

But in other news,
Despite your views,
Your university's not exclusive.
We've all been there,
Had our share of care,
But don't feel the need to get abusive.
We thought the days of name-calling,
So petty and appalling,
Would be left in the schoolyard
With exam grades and report cards.
Who does it help if we fight
To see who was wronged most right,
When we should be righting wrongs,
Not sorting out those who belong
From those who don't.

Major Rager

Standing up for the NHS,
Fighting for the dispossessed,
Honouring those who fought for us,
Caring for those who need it most,
Ignoring those false dichotomies
That suggest we have to limit our sympathies
Between the homeless soldier and the refugees.

We have more in common
Than that which divides us,
More love to go on.
And those that hide from us
The true perpetrators,
The nation's real traitors:
The papers that incite hate,
The lies that hibernate
And rear their heads when memory thaws.
And we forget those years of wars …
As every dog will have its day,
The truth will out and have its say.
When that time comes,
My hand is open
My heart is open
And I will welcome you as brother, sister

Gemma Knowles

Dreams of the Past: A Brexiteer's Mind-set

So what if the economy heads down the pan?
When the brown Brexit shit contacts the fan,
I couldn't give a toss if that is all true:
No bloody foreigner tells me what to do!

So what if Europe could broaden my mind,
Or open horizons make me more refined?
Well bollocks to that and screw the EU.
No bloody foreigner tells me what to do!

So what if the experts all forecast a mess?
I'd rather believe the *Mail* and *Express.*
We don't need the nasty egghead point of view.
No bloody foreigner tells me what to do!

So what if the jobs are all going abroad?
The *Telegraph* says that the forecasts are flawed.
The wops and the frogs will disappear too,
So's no bloody foreigner tells me what to do.

So what if Europe has maintained the peace?
No sodding use if the buggers increase.
Send 'em all back to the feckin' EU!
Then no bloody foreigner tells me what to do.

All them outsiders with a fancy degree:
I don't give a stuff if they're smarter than me.
They can fuck off back home, their families too –
'Cos no bloody foreigner tells me what to do.

Major Rager

Bankers and wankers, remoaners all,
Expats who've deserted make my skin crawl.
They're all bleedin' traitors, rats through and through,
And no bloody foreigner tells me what to do!

Didn't we rule the world and then win the war?
We British are special, for what went before.
I'm a true British patriot, though I haven't a clue
Why no bloody foreigner tells me what to do.

That sums up my feelings on Brexit and stuff.
The *Sun* and the *Mail* say that that's quite enough.
I'm stuck in a time-warp from 1902,
When no bloody foreigner told us what to do.

NL

EU Paradise

As I walk through this Brexit-ridden island of death,
I take a look at Britain and I can see there's little left,
Cos I've been fighting this Brexshit so long
That even my granny thinks that my brain is blown.
But I have never crossed a quitter that wasn't deserving.
Convince me that we should leave, you know that's
unheard of.

I really hate to moan but this ain't no joke.
As they lie I see Britain going up in smoke.
Fools, I'm the kinda Brit that wants to stay a European,
like;
In the pen at Number 10, singing songs in the streetlight.

May says 'strong and stable' and 'Brexit means Brexit.'
If they can't justify it, why should we exit?
You better tell Gove and Boris, and Nigel Farridge
That we won't stop fighting until Brexit is broke.

Look at the messed-up lifestyle that we are facin'.
I can't live a normal life while Brexit's on my mind.
So I gotta fight now with Remain's team:
Too much Brexit talking has messed up my dreams.
I'm an educated girl with the EU on my mind.
Got my flag in my hand and a gleam in my eye.
I'm a pissed-off Remainer, EU flag hanger.
Brexit makes me too mad, so don't inflame my anger.
Fool, Brexit is nothin' but a rigged vote away.
I'm fighting back, do or die, what can I say?
I'm a European now, will I manage to remain one?

Major Rager   Page 54

Prose and Cons – Poems Against The Brexit Machine

The way Brexit's going, I can't know.

They want to stop us from
Livin' in our EU paradise.
We're gonna carry on
Livin' in our EU paradise.

Annie Bell

Granny Remain Says ...

The *Fail*, the *Bun* and the *Distress* just peddle hate and
lies,
And never try to rectify their Brexit bullpoo cries.

The bus with loads of dosh on it, a symbol of the wit
That Farage and his mates spewed out – it was a pile of
shit.

They tried to say they'd took away our sovereignty a bit,
But Queen Eliz she did the biz; they're really talking
sh—
'Ere, did you see 'er 'at?

The poll was rigged: not all could vote – EU citz and
expat Brits.
'We won, you lost, get over it,' the constant chatback
shit.

Our human rights eroding fast; laws changing by the
minute.
They want to kid us that it's fair but it's a crock of shit.

We're even told to leave our homes and clear off out of
it,
But we can't go, cos we won't have no EU citizenship!

Economists, they warned us all of economic drift.
The price of goods is rising; the pound's just gone to shit.

The Irish border's forfeit. Can we cross or not?

Major Rager

Good Friday's lost agreement means we very well may
not.

Was peace for years, free borders and trade not enough
for you?
Now listen well while Granny tells a mote of truth to
you.

If we don't pull together then our country's down the
pan.
A laughing stock is what we are, stupid to a man.

Poll again, don't be a pain, don't be fascist old gits.
Vote Europe IN, stay European, then our country's *out*
the shit.

Why can't you Leavers clear your eyes and open up your
brains,
And listen to the wisdom spouting from Granny Remain?

So follow me and then you'll see, the source of Britain's
pain
Can be reversed through song and verse sung by Granny
Remain.

Lesley Bell

A Lament for Britain

What on earth is happening in my country?
The visionary spark that made it great:
Sure there's plenty good around, but it's all too often drowned
By a rising tide of xenophobic hate.

What the hell is happening in my country?
The atmosphere is like a tribal war.
People don't connect, there's an absence of respect.
The economy is heading for the floor.

What in heaven is happening in my country?
Its tradition of compassion and fair play,
The values that we cherish, will inevitably perish
While governmental witch-hunts rule the day.

What in truth is happening in my country?
Darkness is descending on the nation.
The land that offered hope to those who couldn't cope
Is now engaged in mean recrimination.

What the blazes is happening in my country?
There's a sign of ethnic cleansing on the gate.
Patriotism's blind, it closes down the mind
And opens up the door to racist hate.

What for God's sake is happening in my country?
Why is there so much violence and fear?
Foreigners attacked, their properties sacked,
And sympathy is greeted with a sneer.

Major Rager

What on earth is happening in my country?
Nineteen-thirties fascism's at hand.
The neo-Nazi legions are growing in the regions
And intolerance takes over the land.

What the devil's happening in my country?
Why are all its ideals so deranged?
Education's so inapt that people can't adapt
To a world of transformative change.

What the fuck is happening in my country,
Where the media have robotised the brain?
Few values, sense or reason; thinking's almost treason,
And probity has vanished down the drain.

Please give me back my caring, sharing country,
The one I knew so open and so well.
Give me back the joy I experienced as a boy,
And spare me from this squabbling, blinkered hell.

NL

Sometime in 2019, the K (Formerly the UK)

Goodbye, little island,
Drifting off into the sea.
Fading memories of pink countries, fluttering
desperately,
Your only sail
in the cold winds
of a careless Atlantic.

Little island,
Pleasant pastures,
Leaking power,
lost respect.

Taking back our country
Dulce et decorum est.

Vanessa C. Stone

A Brexit Meltdown

They're pushing hard Brexit.
I doubt we'll fare well,
Cos Mayhem has screwed us
with hard Brexit hell.
I guess that Farage is to blame
for gaining ground (gaining ground).
Britain will never be the same again.

It's a Brexit meltdown,
A Brexit meltdown.

Brexit's a shit sandwich,
A great load of poo.
A hard or soft Brexit,
It's still made of poo,
With so many nightmares to fight
And lies to be countered (to be countered).
If not then this country is screwed.

It's a Brexit meltdown,
A Brexit meltdown.

Annie Bell

All About EU (No Brexit)

> Yeah, it's obvious, I love the EU.
> And I'll fight Brexit, the way I mean to do,
> Cos I've had enough of listening to Leavers' shit:
> Shouting, 'We won, you lost, now get over it.'
>
> We hear those Brexshitters
> 'wanting their country back'.
> We know they were lied to.
> They'd better take it back.
> If you love Europe,
> Then listen to my call:
> That Brexit don't mean Brexit.
> Let's remain in the EU!
>
> You know those Leavers were shafted,
> And sold a shed-load of lies.
> And on that basis Treeza decided to cut all ties.
> I guess that makes her a Brexshit, EU-quitting
> Neanderthal.
> And I hate what she's into, so I'm gonna carry on
> Fighting Brexit.
>
> Give us our EU back.
> Please tell those rotten Brexit bitches that
> We want our country back!
> But I'm here to let you know
> That Brexit don't mean Brexit.
> Let's remain in the EU!

Annie Bell

Major Rager

Name of the Beast

>
Dictators come and dictators go,
a title never lost in the passage of time

some may whisper haltingly
about genius economic policies

or the instilling of national pride,

but it matters not.
history will always have the last word:

a dictator is as a dictator does,
now and for ever.

Marc Perry

Evidence Blocked

The impact studies would enlighten debate
On the wisdom of risking our country's fate;
So why are they not being put up on view
So everyone knows what they're signing up to?

Brexit's the biggest challenge we face:
It affects our lives in so many ways;
So why isn't the evidence of Brexit's impacts
Being published to give every Briton the facts?

While our government persists to refuse,
We can only believe that it isn't good news.
And if that's the case, shouldn't we all learn
That Brexit's a major national concern?

And shouldn't the government do what it can
To reverse toxic policy and cancel the plan?
Or is it the prisoner of backers with means,
Who pull all the strings to fulfil their schemes?

Whatever, there is no earthly excuse
To keep all its citizens ignorant of truths.
That's not democracy, it's manipulation
That transforms Great Britain to a small-minded
nation.

NL

EU Superheroes

> Maddie Kay and Steven Bray,
> Making history every day.
> Our wise campaign to Remain
> Chips away at Treeza May.
>
> One day we'll hear Leavers say
> They're glad that Brexit's gone away.
> Our wise campaign to Remain
> Proved the EU is OK.

Helen Cooney

Letters to Europe

Dear Europe, we want to send a letter to you.
You might not read it, but it's something that we
have to do!
There's so many things that we've got to say;
If we put it down on paper, perhaps you'll read it
someday?

Dear Europe, these are our letters to you,
Delivered by hand, across a sea so blue,
Written with love and sealed with care,
To show solidarity we hope is still there.

They tried to part us and told us things that just
weren't true.
They won their vote based upon dishonest
misconceptions of you.
So here is our apology. We hope you can forgive.
A world without unity is not a place that we want
to live.

Dear Europe, these are our letters to you ...

No borders too high, no waters too wide –
Can't you see the torment that we're feeling
inside?
Prejudice and hate won't stand in our way,
Or stop us from saying what we've got to say.

Dear Europe, these are our letters to you,
Golden stars on a flag of blue.

Madeleina Kay

Merry Maytime

In the merry time of May,
Ministers come out to play.
They fill the land with noisy Babel,
Mislead as much as they are able.

In the merry time of May,
Some say 'Leave' and some say 'stay'.
Let us be clear, this is no fable,
With government so strong and stable.

In the merry time of May,
Globalise – make lots of hay.
And proud, our leaders thump the table,
Believe the pound is strong and stable.

In the merry time of May,
They'll lose votes now, if we stay.
They've got a mandate – they can flex it,
While rushing swiftly for an exit.

In the merry time of May,
Negotiations are the way.
No need for planning round a table:
Our government is strong and stable.

In the merry time of May,
Everyone is made to pay.
'Less immigration' is the label
Written by the strong and stable.

Major Rager   Page 67

In the merry time of May,
Will Scots leave, or will they stay?
Hard indecision lamentable
But May is here, so strong and stable.

In the merry time of May,
Ireland's peace begins to fray ...
But leprechauns with magic cable
Ensure a border, strong and stable.

In the merry time of May,
Riches slowly drain away.
But government is always able
New deals to find: it's strong and stable.

In the merry time of May,
With promised deal one happy day;
The very best that's ever done –
A deal that works for ev'ryone!

Or in the merry time of May,
It may be 'No deal's best' they say.
No big deal for those who're able
To believe the strong and stable.

In the merry time of May,
When Brussels sprouts are put away,
We're strong and stable, always able
With home-grown food to deck the table.

In the merry time of May,
Party whips are used, they say.

Major Rager

They crack their whips when May's unable
To find support for strong and stable.

And when May's days are frayed and done,
We'll see that they were never fun.
Because an exit hard and knobbly
Has brought a Maytime weak and wobbly.

So better stop the exodus,
That long and lacquered bright-red bus.
Where Maytime untruth too far goes
To bring on us the worst of woes.

Peter St John

Referendum Denier

So, people start to call us Referendum deniers,
Cos we won't respect a vote that was stolen by liars.
What you gonna call us when Brexit backfires?
What you gonna do when the upshot transpires?

Referendum denier, Referendum denier –
Is that like flat-earth denier?
That like climate-change denier?
That like Holocaust denier?
Evolution denier?
Can't you get it any higher
Than to call me a denier?
Cos I won't respect a vote
That was stolen by liars?

So, yeah, I'm gonna *own* 'Referendum denier'.
I deny we can't speak, when we're the only ones awake.
I deny we can't turn back, when we're making a mistake.
I deny I'll let our freedoms disappear without a fight.
I deny people can vote away our hard-won rights.
I deny that democracy can function when we're blind.
I deny that our electorate can never change its mind.
I deny that 'the People's will' is never ever wrong.
I deny a man can say that his neighbour 'can't belong'.
I deny our press should be allowed to teach us how to
hate.
I deny our MPs should just shut up and abdicate.
I deny that our country should be run by plebiscite.
I deny I'm not a patriot, for wanting what is right.

Jane Berry

Intolerance

The sun has set
on the glory days of civilisation,
of men having dreams,

the steel jaws of ignorance
clamping down on humanity
and refusing to withdraw.

'Let us fear that which is other;
that which is not me':
words echoing round
an empty-headed world.

'What I do not understand must be feared.'
The bigot speaks
with a gun-muzzle mouth,

hot-lead death,
fanatical rhetoric.

I am intolerant of intolerance,
of the blinkered hiding behind
their patriotic pride,

Deaf ears scattering the words of the wise
To lie broken,
Trampled underfoot.

I see no reason to tolerate this.

I see no reason.

Marc Perry

Major Rager

Marching for Europe

Got up this morning, and my plan is that I'll fight.
I plan to fight so hard, to stay in the EU.
I will go out, I'll catch the tube to Marble Arch,
and I will join the march to stay in the EU.
I'll wave my blue flag with its ring of golden stars,
I'll wave it hard so we can stay in the EU.
Bollocks to Brexit! They're the words that I will shout.
Yes I will shout so hard to stay in the EU.

I'll be thinking of the things the EU does,
Of all the things the EU does for me and you:
It gives us freedom, freedom to live, work and retire,
And to get healthcare anywhere in the EU.
It supports business, it boosts our economic state,
and offers social support to people who're in need.
The EU protects, it protects our human rights,
and it protects our health and safety laws as well.

And that's not all now. The EU does lots more besides.
You won't believe how much we get for fifty quid.
That's why I'm marching and I'll march and march again.
I'm gonna march so much to stay in the EU.
I'll wave my blue flag with its ring of golden stars,
I'll wave it hard so we can stay in the EU.
Bollocks to Brexit! They're the words that I will shout.
Yes I will shout so hard to stay in the EU.

Annie Bell

Pink Pig

I saw a pink pig on Saturday –
Don't know how he got there –
Kept shouting, 'Brexit is Brexit is Brexit,'
As if it were a mystical prayer.

I asked him why Brexit is Brexit.
He said, 'Sovereignty, sovereignty' twice.
So I said, 'But we've always had sovereignty!'
And he disappeared in a trice.

I met a blue elephant on Sunday –
Don't know where from or when –
Kept shouting 'Borders and borders and borders!'
Over and over again.

I asked, 'Why borders and borders?
There are queues after airline flights
Cos we've always preserved our borders.'
So he soon disappeared out of sight.

I saw a white monkey on Monday.
He had an old atlas in tow.
Kept shouting, 'Empire and empire and empire!
We British are special, you know.'

So I told him the empire is over:
We trade with our neighbours today.
They are the source of our real wealth –
So he cursed me and just went away.

On Tuesday I met a red camel –
By now I was starting to freak –
Kept shouting, 'NHS, NHS, NHS,
Three-fifty million per week!'

So I asked what happened to the promise
Emblazoned all over the bus.
He said he didn't know where it went to,
And vamoosed with no time to discuss.

On Wednesday I saw a green donkey –
It popped up into my view –
Droning, 'Will of the people, the people,
It's time to leave the EU.'

So I asked him, 'Which will of the people?
The one that applied to last year,
Or the one that polls tell us has changed now?'
So he vanished into thin air.

A yellow cow met me on Thursday –
This really is a strange week –
Shouted, 'Democracy and more democracy:
The people have voted to speak!'

So I asked, 'What's meant by democracy?
Does it exclude the 48 per cent?
And what happens if that becomes 60?'
Well he couldn't work out what I meant.

On Friday a purple Gove-bill
Flew into the upstairs spare room,

Shouting, 'No experts, no experts, no experts:
No more expressions of gloom!'

I asked him, 'What's wrong with experts?'
He said that they always tell lies.
'Read the *Mail* and the *Sun* and *Express*
If you really want to be wise.'

And that just sums up my last week:
Stranger and stranger each day.
When challenged, the Brexit supporters
All seemed to melt right away.

NL

The Apologist (Administrative Cock-up)

They sent the letters out.
She read it, crying in her teacup.
The suitcases were full now;
There was nothing more to pack up.
Those lives our vote destroyed:
Yeah – just administrative cock-up.

The farmer sold the fields,
And yeah, he's been and sold the stock up.
It turns out there was no one there
To pick the rotten crop up.
The livelihoods we wrecked:
Yeah – just administrative cock-up.

The factory is quiet now,
They had another shake-up.
The jobs are gone, the market's dead,
There hasn't been a let-up.
It went downhill, but
Mostly, just administrative cock-up

It's hard to get my treatment now;
I need to ring the doc up.
I need something called isotopes;
It's hard for them to stock up.
So, you know what it just sounds like?
Yeah: administrative cock-up.

I miss my holidays in Spain.
The flight costs are a shocker.

Major Rager   Page 76

It's all so complicated now,
You can't just sort of rock up.
Don't know why they shut Ryanair:
Administrative cock-up.

My pension won't support me now.
I work, to get a top-up.
It's not the pound that's crashed,
It's just they messed the triple lock up.
My politics don't make me poor:
Administrative cock-up.

The hatred on the streets –
Those sort of people you should lock up.
I don't know why it all kicked off.
I'm not a racist bloke, but
The way it all turned out,
Yeah, pure administrative cock-up.

Jane Berry

Prose and Cons – Poems Against The Brexit Machine

Let's Take Control

Let's take control from that no-good EU!
Let's make everyone join a long queue,
Make sure the airports stand as our sentry,
Make sure that passports are shown upon entry.

Let's make the seaports good and secure.
Let's take control and keep Britain pure.
Keep out the foreigners who aren't like us:
Let's make 'em suffer if they make a fuss.

Good that the Channel's between us and them,
Or we'd have had Schengen from God-knows-when.

Hold on a minute – I just had a thought.
This line of thinking is coming to nought.

Passports *are* needed at each entry place.
We're doing what we've always done in any case.
Queues are much longer but still in good order,
So what's all this crap about controlling our border?

Just wait till we're in WTO rules:
That's when we'll know we've been taken for fools.
Extra tariffs to encourage compliance
While the rest of world trades in profitable alliance.

NL

Limerick Corner

There is a new system called Brexit,
Which takes a proud nation and wrecks it.
Experts said it won't work,
But the government berks
Said, 'We're stuffed cos we can't find an exit.'

Vicki Harris

There was a mad doctor called Fox
Who'd put the EU in the stocks.
You wouldn't believe it:
He thought he'd achieve it
By throwing us all on the rocks.

A certain ambitious buffoon
Wants to be PM quite soon.
To achieve his ambition,
He'd practise sedition;
But he's just a big windbag balloon.

NL

There was an old woman called Treeza
Who teamed up with untrustworthy geezers
To impose a con trick
(Voted for by the thick),
Though it never could be a crowd pleaser.

Vicki Harris

A party not fond of isonomy
Wanted Brexit autonomy.
To make it all happen
They'd use any weapon
To ruin the British economy.

NL

There was a blond man of ambition
Who took his homeland to perdition.
He cried, 'Folks, don't panic!
We're on the Titanic –
My success of a sinking-ship mission.'

Vicki Harris

There is a Bullingdon buffoon
Thinks he'll be prime minister soon.
But this elegant scheme
Will be just a dream
If we all recognise he's a loon.

NL

Songs

If Brexit be the food of death, play on

Music reaches us in ways that spreadsheets cannot. No wonder we were told to vote with our hearts and not our heads. Now we have the benefit of hindsight, we are beginning to see what a gross act of socio-economic self-harm Brexit is. I have used music throughout my life as a means of reaching people's heads, hearts and souls through my work as a business academic and keynote speaker. It is indeed more effective than a spreadsheet or PowerPoint graphic as a direct route of administration into our hearts. I began my activism as the musical director for the No. 10 Vigil. This group campaigns tirelessly opposite Downing Street to highlight EU benefits and Brexit fantasies. At No. 10, rather than dumbing down to the level of the populist press, we decided to 'dumb up' our approach by combining intelligent thinking with music to reach people's heads, hearts and souls. We found our voice by rewriting songs that are ripe for what I've termed Brexitosis, where lyrics are bent or broken to fit particular Brexit stories of the day. Our repertoire included daring rewrites of classics such as Bachman Turner Overdrive's 'You Ain't Seen Brexit Yet', about David Davis' negotiating strategies: 'Any Brexit is good Brexit ... so I took what I could get'.

Bruno Mars' 'Uptown Funk' was rewritten as a personal confessional by our Boris Johnson impersonator. Pink Floyd's 'Another Prick in The Mall' was prompted by the rock band I started with former Bank of England committee member Dr Andrew Sentance. One crowd favourite is David Bowie's 'Brexit Oddity'. The inspiration came in the shower as I mused that Brexit is like going into space with no plan for the destination or the journey. Bowie's newly warped words blasted out on the street at Theresa May's hustings in Maidenhead as she drove past in her Jaguar:

'Ground Control to Theresa May, take your HRT and put your heels away ...'

'Brexit Oddity' even inspired the CEO of a charity to rewrite the Peter Sarstedt classic 'Where Do You Go to, My Lovely':

'You live in a fancy apartment, Off the Boulevard of Whitehall, Where you craft your Kafkaesque soundbites, With a fiend called Gavin Barwell. They say that when you got married, It was to fleece a trillionaire. But they don't realise you're from Eastbourne, And I wonder if they really care, or give a damn, ah ha ha ha.'

Many other willing contributors have added songs, and their work is given space in this part of the book. Our approach helps people find their voice to Remain. Rock 'n' roll is the ultimate voice of the people, so the last words must go to my friend Bernie Tormé, the Dublin-bred former guitarist for Ozzy Osbourne and Ian Gillan:

'Brexit is doing to this country what the iceberg did to the *Titanic*. It's a total disaster, economically, socially and politically. One saving grace of being on the

Titanic was that the crew didn't witter on to the punters that it was the will of the passengers that the iceberg had to be steered into. Or that total belief in a rosy outcome would keep the ship afloat. Fantasy island, meet iceberg.'

Peter Cook

Sky, Sun Still Maligning
to the tune of 'Hi Ho Silver Lining'

Your Brexit's going nowhere, Murdoch, that's where
we're at.
You're going down the hill since Hillsborough, with that
Kelvin Twat.
Trying to wreck the country, you plutocrat,
Saying everything's the EU's fault, for your *coup d'etat*!

And it's Sky, *Sun*, still maligning
Every EU story, baby.
We see the *Sun* is lying:
It don't take a bus,
Cos it's obvious.

Lies are gonna get you some day, just wait and see.
Your rag's for racists, Murdoch, the *Scum*'s not for me.
The Liverpool boycott's groovy: No-*Sun* City.
Your Sky's the limit, Murdoch: we'll stop watching TV!

And it's Sky, *Sun*, ...

Jane Berry

Pants to Brexit

[Chant:]
Give us a thong, give us a thong,
Now I see where we went wrong.
Exit Brexit: it's a stitch up,
All we want's a thong for Europe.

[Chorus:]
Brexit, I thought you would excite me –
Strong control pants hugging me tightly –
Now I see that you're just unsightly.
We don't want no, no tighty-whitey.

[Rap:]
Brexit, I thought you'd excite me –
Strong control pants hug me tightly.
Brexit's coming back to bite me.
Now we need to save old Blighty!

Brexit exit ain't denied me:
I can change with truth to guide me.
We know now the other side, they
Lied, they lied, they lied, they fried me.

[Chorus:]
Brexit, I thought you would excite me ...

[Rap:]
Now the choice is fight or flight. We
See the iceberg on the Right. We
Got to make a move tonight. We

Gonna fall into the white sea.

Captain Corbeye might be right? He
Left us jumping into ice. He
Told us we would be all right, he
Brexit pants would save my life.

[Chant:]
Brexit, you won't give us the edge, see:
All we're getting here is a tight-arsed wedgie.
Hear the beat, it's rock-unsteady.
Seen the scene, it just looks deadly.

[Rap:]
Captain Corbeye gave me a fright: free-
dom of movement outta sight. He
Brexit pants are full of shite. He
Just the same as May almighty.

It's Titanic – woe betide me:
All my rights are now denied me!
We goin' down on the Brexit tide, we
Know it's time that Brexit died. Hey!

Jane Berry

If You Only Had a Heart

This world is built from insanity and glass,
Where power-hungry egos create the indignity of
class.
Values built on privilege, wealth and greed
Create hierarchies that perpetuate our needs.

But when we shine the light, your illusions
will smash,
And your empires will crumble amidst piles of
your burning cash.
And we will forge our futures based on different
priorities.
And we will work together as unified societies.

If you only had a heart,
If you only had a heart,
You would realise how it feels
To tear us all apart!

I won't stand for this, no, no!
I would never let my morals stoop to points so
low.
We are the opposition and we will fight
For what we know is true and what we know
is right.

If you only had a heart ...

Madeleina Kay

That Dirty Maggie May

to the tune of 'Maggie Mae'

Now gather round me, bonny boys, and listen to my
plea.
And when you've heard my sorry tale, I'm sure you'll
pity me:
For I was taken down on the streets of London town,
On the first day that I come home from the sea.

I was thrust upon the dole, where I stood behind a Pole,
Just four pound ten a week, that was my pay.
But though ragged, poor and thin, I was very soon took
in
By a harlot with the name of Maggie May.

Oh that dirty Maggie May, they have taken her away,
And she'll never walk up Downing Street no more
With her six-inch heels a-clickin' and her sights on tight
spring chicken,
That dirty, robbin', no-good Maggie May.

Now I well recall the day when I first met Maggie May;
She was cruising up and down on Hampton Wick.
She'd a face so cold and snow-like, and a manner cruel
and crow-like,
But me, I'm just a Quitter, and I'm thick.

She took me up to bed, whereupon she sweetly said
That if I trusted her then she'd be mine.

Why, with her so strong and stable, and me so young and able,
Our future life together would be fine!

Oh that dirty Maggie May, they have taken her away,
And she'll never walk down Downing Street no more.
For she robbed me sweet and stealthy just to give it to the wealthy,
That dirty, robbin', no-good Maggie May.

In the morning when I woke, I was flat and stony broke:
No jacket, kecks nor wallet could be found.
When I asked her where they were, she said, 'You halfwit cur,
They're for the boat and halfway Brussels-bound.'

Swift to Dover I did run, but of my clothing found I none.
So the voters came and took that girl away.
And the judge he guilty found her, of robbing a homeward-bounder,
And I think meself well lucky to this day.

Oh that dirty Maggie May, they have taken her away,
And a curse upon her party evermore.
Oh hearken to my story and never trust a Tory
Like that dirty, robbin', no-good Maggie May.

Peter Roberts

The Battle Hymn of the Trumpeduplic
to the tune of 'Battle Hymn of the Republic'

He's a rootin' tootin' racist, on that we're all agreed.
Appeals to white supremacists and the neo-Nazi creed.
He's a bigoted self-publicist and a paragon of greed,
And Trump goes marching on.

Glory glory hallelujah,
Donald Trump is trying to screw ya.
It's enough to make you spew, yeah,
But Trump goes marching on.

No constructive policies for purposeful debate,
Just plain destructive fallacies and the politics of hate.
Reasonable Republicans can surely not relate
As Trump goes marching on.

Glory glory …

He's a model of intolerance and he's arrogant and vain,
Stupefying ignorance of what earth can sustain.
Those who cast their vote for him must never use their
brain
As the chump goes marching on.

Glory glory …

A war chest full of money bought his way to power,
And homophobic honey helped his campaign to flower.
If he ever comes to England, we'll send him to the
Tower,

As Trump goes marching on.

Glory glory ...

Terrorists are delighted he views Muslims all the same.
They know that he has blighted his own country's noble
name.
Intelligent Americans just hang their heads in shame
As Trump goes marching on.

Glory glory ...

Now this prick's become the President there is suffering
worldwide.
It's not a good advertisement for America's self-pride.
The most predicted outcome will be global suicide
As Trump goes marching on.

Glory glory hallelujah,
Donald Trump is trying to screw ya.
It's enough to make you spew, yeah,
The arsehole goes marching on.

NL

No, Jeremy Corbyn

He looks like Jesus Christ,
He cooks basmati rice.
JC will rip it up,
Taking hard Brexit on, come what May.

And I recall the lies on the bus.
The wheels went round and round.
Riding high on Virgin Trains,
No cheap seats to be found.
And the words coming from Jezza's beard
Say 'Leave the EU.'

No, Jeremy Corbyn [x4],
Don't wanna hear that Brexshit.
Every MP's got too much baggage:
No one stands up to Brexshit,
From Donald Trump to Nigel Farridge.

And if I catch Jezza coming my way,
I'm gonna shout, 'No, no, no!'
And if JC don't want to hear,
I say he's got to go, go go.
No way, Jeremy Corbyn,
Just stop the soft Brexit spin.

Goin' to Islington –
Long way from Bridlington.
He's gonna whip 'em all,
Make red Tories sweat votes out of the poor.

Major Rager   Page 92

And I'm bleeding Old Labour blood
From Michael's Foot
In the House of Lords.
Momentum's gonna suck my soul dry,
And you will eat your damson pie.
And voices coming from my brain
Tell me to Remain.

No, Jeremy Corbyn [x4]

Peter Cook

@albawhitewolf

Another Prick in The Mall

We don't need no consultation,
We don't need no press control,
No dark sarcasm in the Commons.
Leavers, leave snowflakes alone!
Hey! Mayhem! Leave our kids alone.
All in all you're just another prick in The Mall.
All in all you're just another prick in The Mall.

We don't need no reformation,
We don't need media control,
No dark sarcasm in the House of Lords.
Leavers, leave snowflakes alone!
Hey! Mayhem! Leave our kids alone!
All in all you're just another prick in The Mall.
All in all you're just another prick in The Mall.

Punk Floyd (a.k.a. Peter Cook)

Daisy Davis
to the tune of 'Daisy Bell'

David Davis, give me your answer do.
Are you crazy, to think that we'll leave the EU?
The vote was a huge miscarriage, we can't trust Nigel
Farridge.
And May looks sick cos the deal's Brexshit, and you
really don't have a clue.

David Davis, give me your answer do:
Referenda, you said in two thousand and two,
'Don't vote on a blank sheet of paper, and fill in the
details later.'
Did you change your mind or did you find that
Parliament's there to screw?

David Davis, give me your answer do:
How's Fox and Boris? Are they getting along with you?
The three stooges together, not one can tell us whether
A deal for trade will ever be made with Korea or
Timbuktu.

David Davis, give me your answer do:
Last September, you said they'd be in a queue:
From the Commonwealth to China, Brazil to Asia Minor.
So, let's sell bombs and arms and guns to a nasty
dictator or two.

David Davis, give me your answer do:
What's the plan now you're talking with the EU?

Major Rager   Page 95

You've got your sixty studies – but we've got no global buddies.
It's got quite late to negotiate, and May now expects a coup.

Jane Berry

Granny Remain's Rap to Old Brexiters

I'm Granny Remain. We olds ain't all the same.
I voted to stay European that day.
I don't want no Brexit society,
So I'll run in me bloomers, lose all sense of propriety,
Get attention for the cause by acting all flighty,
Until the Leavers see sense and do what's right for old
Blighty.

You other old folks who voted to leave,
You'll be long dead and gone and leave your young uns
to grieve,
Cos you voted out, making Great Britain heave
Its way out of the EU and drop us all in the poo.

The pound's gone to shit, folks are leaving Great Brit-
An I just want to say, don't treat us this way!
Cos it's making me mad, making me bad-assed.
There ain't nothing you can say to make me change my
ways,
Cos I know that I am right and I'm up for the fight.

So don't tell me, 'We won, you lost, get over it,'
Cos I ain't taking any more of your shit.
Do the right thing, let's have another vote.
You'll be surprised; look and see through their lies,
Then the status quo might just be revived.

Lesley Bell

Brexit RIP
to the tune of 'Oh Susanna'

The banks are leaving daily, here they cannot stay,
And industry is terrified their market's flown away.
Oh, poor Britain, poverty's here to stay.
Brexit's a disaster on every single day.

Investment into Britain's low and jobs are falling free.
They want five hundred million markets, not just six
point three.
Oh, poor Britain, you know what you must do:
You'd better cancel Brexit before it cancels you.

Britain is a laughing stock, it's committing suicide.
The likelihood of self-destruction cannot be denied.
Oh, poor Britain, led by feeble May,
You're bankrupting your country in a strong and stable
way.

The tabloid press is trying hard to camouflage the truth,
But nothing they can say will hide disaster for our youth.
Oh, poor Britain, how long can this last?
Britain's in the process of self-destructing fast.

People now have changed their minds, they know that
they were conned.
Now they wait impatiently for your government to
respond.
Oh, poor Britain, it all comes down to you:
There's now a good majority to stay in the EU.

Major Rager

Your options now are fading fast, they're not hard to see:
On the one hand your rich billionaires, on the other
bankruptcy.
Oh, poor Britain, pride comes before a fall.
You must kill off the Brexit wreck before it wrecks us all.

NL

The End of Our Hopes
to the tune of 'Delilah'

We saw the end of our hopes and our dreams in June 16.
We knew the the people were tricked but it was now too
late.
They read the tabloids:
They were all poisoned against migrants, and sealed our
fate.

What a waste, losing nurses!
They're off back home, muttering curses.
All our wealth makers, our doctors, EMA, farmers:
They are all buggered, in need of a May money tree.

We have been fighting, protesting and even remoaning.
We must save our NHS and other good things.
Leavers are mocking:
They all believe that Brexit will give the nation wings.

What a mess, losing ...

Give it some thought, and keep your EU passport!
Your freedom of movement is worth fighting for.
Yes, freedom of movement is worth fighting for!

What a fate, losing ...

Vicki Harris

Prose and Cons – Poems Against The Brexit Machine

Part of the EU

to the tune of 'Part of the Union'

Now I'm an EU fan, amazed at what I am.
I say what I think, that Brexit stinks. Yes, I'm an EU fan.
When we meet outside No 10, which is really near Big Ben,
With a hell of a shout, it's 'Brexit out!'
And we sing to the government's den.

As a European I'm wise to the lies of the Brexit spies,
And I don't get fooled by the government rules
Cos I always read between the lines.
And I always get my way when I fight to have my say.
I'm scrapping hard to mark Brexit's card and this is what I
say:

Oh, you won't stop me, I'm part of the EU,

You won't stop me, I'm part of the EU,
You won't stop me, I'm part of the EU
Till the day I die.

Before the EU did appear, my life was half as clear.
Now I've got the power to the working hour,
And every other day of the year.

So though I'm an ancient gran, I can ruin the government's
plan;
And though it's absurd and Brexit's a turd,
We're a multi-aged super-clan.

Oh, you won't stop me ...

Lesley Bell

Major Rager

Where Do EU Go to, My Lovely?

You talk like Werner von Blomberg,
And you dress like a sartorial wreck.
Your clothes are all made by Peacocks,
And there's diamonds and bling round your neck.

You live in a fancy apartment
Off the boulevard of Whitehall,
Where you craft your Kafkaesque soundbites
With a fiend called Gavin Barwell, yes you do.

But where do you go to, Theresa,
When you're tucked up in your bed?
Tell me the lies that surround you;;
I want to look inside your head.

I've seen all your qualifications
You bought from Oxford dons,
And the catchphrase you stole from the Fuhrer ('strong
and stable').
Your duplicity goes on and on, yes it does.

Major Rager

Prose and Cons – Poems Against The Brexit Machine

When you go on your summer vacation,
You tend to run through wheat fields
In your red, white and blue Brexit swimsuit,

You run and run through the fields, in leather pants, in
kitten heels, ah, ha ha ha.

When the snow falls you're found at the G7
With the others of the rich set,
While the proletariat raid food banks
And students get deeper in debt: yes they do, pathetic
fools, ha ha ha ha ha.

But where do you go to, Theresa,
When you're fucked up in your head?
Tell me your dreams from the wheat fields;
I want to look inside your bed, yes I do.

Your name is cursed in high places.
You know Jean-Claude Juncker:
He sent a walking stick for Brexit,
And you keep it just for fun, for a laugh, for walks in
wheat fields, ah ha ha ha.

Major Rager

They say that when you got married
It was to fleece a trillionaire.
But they don't realise you're from Eastbourne,
And I wonder if they really care, or give a damn, ship of
fools, ah ha ha ha.

But where do you go to, Theresa,
When you're tucked up in your bed?
Tell me the lies that surround you;
I want to look inside your head, yes I do.

I remember the back streets of Hastings:
Old people begging in rags,
Drinking cans of Carlsberg Special
To shake off their lowly brown tags, yes they try, ah ha
ha.

So look into my face, Theresa May,
And remember just who you are –
Then go and forget me for ever.
Cos I know you still bear the scar, deep inside, yes you
do.

Major Rager

I know where you go to, Theresa,
When you're drowning in Brexshit.
I know the lies that surround you.
Look, love, it's time that you quit.

Peter Sarcasm

The Three Brexiteers
to the tune of 'The Battle Hymn of the Republic'

They charmed the right-wing Tories and the neo-Nazi
youth,
They sought out all the weak ones with the cunning of a
sleuth,
They told enormous whoppers as if it were the truth:
That's the three Brexiteers.

Glory glory halleleujah,
Brexiteers are out to screw ya.
Doesn't it make you want to spew, yeah,
As they go marching on?

They appeal to older people who cannot cope with
change,
And to the tabloid readers for whom thinking is so
strange.
The hateful views of Donald Trump are well within the
range
Of the three Brexiteers.

Glory glory hallelujah,
Immigration is their brew, yeah.
Xenophobia will win through, yeah,
As they go marching on.

They dish out all the half-truths with a smile that seems
sincere,
They spread the myths on Europe, as much as they can
smear.

Major Rager   Page 106

They know that conning people will profit their career:
That's the three Brexiteers.

Glory glory halleliujah,
Welcome to the racist zoo, yeah.
Join the chauvinistic queue, yeah,
With the three Brexiteers.

They know that British people are patriotic guys,
So they showed the Europeans as devils in disguise.
The credulous and gullible all believed the lies
Of the three Brexiteers.

Glory glory hallelujah,
What was true is now untrue, yeah.
They think that we don't have a clue, yeah,
Do the three Brexiteers.

For jingoistic politics of hate this is their hour.
They've hoodwinked British citizens to find their way to
power.
They'll bankrupt the economy to reach the golden
tower,
Will the three Brexiteers.

Glory glory hallelujah,
They do just what they have to do, yeah,
To land the country in the poo, yeah.
That's the three Brexiteers.

NL

The Brexit Blues
to the tune of 'Heartbreak Hotel'

Well I watch the bankers off to Frankfurt,
And the jobs are gonna bust.
And it's all down to the Brexiteers,
So I think then that I must
Be gettin' the Brexit blues, baby,
Yeah, I've got those old Brexit blues.
There ain't no gettin' over
Those old Brexit blues.

Well the pound's gone down the Swannee,
Prices are in the skies.
The country can't take much more shit
Because of Brexit's lies.
And I get those Brexit blues, baby,
Yeah, those old Brexit blues.
There ain't no gettin' over
We'll be at the back of the queue.

Well I listen to those Brexit boys,
And it drives me to despair.
They're livin' in a la-la land
That simply isn't there.
So I get the Brexit blues, baby,
Yeah, those old Brexit blues.
There ain't no gettin' over
What they say just ain't darn true.

Well Brexit's simply crazy,

Major Rager   Page 108

It poisons the nation through.
But those stupid Brexiteers
They just don't have a clue.
Let's play the Brexit blues, baby,
Just for one last time,
Before we all end up
Drownin' in the Brexit slime.

Oh yeah.

NL

Whiskey in the Jar

As I was a goin' over the Cork and Kerry mountains,
I met with Captain Farage, and his money he was counting.
I first produced my pistol and I then produced my rapier;
I said stand or deliver or the devil he may take ya.

Mush-a ring dumb-a do dumb-a da,
Whack fall, my daddy-o, whack fall, my daddy-o,
There's whiskey in the jar-o.

I counted out his money and it made a pretty penny.
I put it in me pocket and I took it home to Treeza.
She swore that she'd love me, never would she leave me;
But the devil take that woman, for you know she tricked me easy.

Mush-a ring dumb-a do dumb-a da ...

Being drunk and weary, I went to Treeza's chamber,
Takin' my money with me, and I never knew the danger.
For about six or maybe seven in walked Captain Farage.
I jumped up, fired off my pistols and I shot him with both barrels.

Mush-a ring dumb-a do dumb-a da ...

Prose and Cons – Poems Against The Brexit Machine

Now some men like the Leavin', and some men like
Remainin',

And some men like ta hear a cannonball a roarin'.
Me? I like sleepin', specially in Treeza's chamber.
But here I am in prison, with a Brexit ball and chain,
yeah.

The Brexiteers (a.k.a. Peter Cook)

Brexiteria
to the tune of 'It's a Long Way to Tipperary'

Pack up the Brexit in your old kit bag and smile, smile, smile.
Send it to Lucifer in an old bag, or drown it in the Nile.
What's the use of Brexit now it's really not worth while?
So
Pack up the Brexit in your old kit bag and smile, smile, smile.

It's a long way to tip a Brexit, it's a long way to go.
It's a long way to tip a Brexit, but it must be done right now.
If not, goodbye Britain, farewell jobs galore.
It's a long long way to tip a Brexit, but show it the door.

NL

May Trip to Florence
to the tune of 'Day Trip to Bangor'

Didn't we have a lovely time the day we went to
Florence?
A beautiful day, I'd a hunch on the way it all might
bugger the pound, you know.
To fill out the pack I invited the hacks; I've got to keep
them on side –ah!
Sling in a few of my vapid harangues, as the wheels fall
off.

Do you recall the killer: we all just bummed it off the
taxpayer:
The flights, the hotel, the church hall as well, was all a
fiddly-scam, you know.
Boris and me hid our enmity, while I mentioned 2020;
Kicking the can down the road, if we can, as the wheels
fall off.

Boris and me, said Brexiters, see, we'd never felt at
home there.
Britain wants links, but nobody thinks it just might be a
shame to go.
It'd really be grand to have all our demands and to stay
like this for always.
The trade, the defence: we'll sit on the fence while the
wheels fall off.

While Europe is nice, we don't like the price. It's not our
national story.

Major Rager   Page 113

We're special and deep so we want it all cheap – or we'll just copy what you have got.
The Irish are fine, they'll step into line: an imaginative border.
We're partners, its true – so it's over to you, as the wheels fall off.

Jane Berry

Humoresque
to the tune of Dvořák's Humoresque No. 7

If you ever hear of Brexit, make your way toward the
exit.
Brexit is a toxic kind of brew.
It uses pure intimidation to bankrupt Britain as a nation
And sends employment spinning out of view.

Brexit, oh Brexit , what's the use of Brexit?
Brexit's daft from every point
Of view-ew-ew.

Politicians on the make, don't worry if their truth is fake.
They target the weak-minded people first,
But the thing they never tell, the consequence is worse
than hell,
And they're the ones who'll always come off worst.

Brexit, oh Brexit ...

Backed by billionaires who need to save and multiply
their greed,
And use their wealth and tabloids to persuade;
It only takes a little thought to see their readers have
been bought:
They're feeding off the people they've betrayed.

Brexit, oh Brexit ...

Where you get your information is a key consideration:
The press isn't shy of doctoring the news.

They're owned by foreign billionaires, the tale they spin
to you is theirs;
Their interest's more in power and moulding views.

Brexit, oh Brexit …

Big decisions need reflection, shouldn't be based on
disaffection;
The facile path's much easier to find.
Nationalism's strident call is an option for us all,
But it tends to close down openness of mind.

Brexit, oh Brexit …

World economies are fragile in a world that's ever
hostile,
So we need an informed point of view.
Taking needless risks is chancy, so let's leave the flights
of fancy
To the dorks who rarely think things through.

Brexit, oh Brexit …

Foreign firms invest in Britain for its singular position
In Europe's half-a-billion marketplace.
That's a million jobs adrift, when those wise investors
shift
Their business to a European base.

Brexit, oh Brexit …

The pound's already in the drink because we simply

didn't think
The consequences would be so extreme.
The most successful nations know their trade and
affluence will grow
When working with each other as a team.

Brexit, oh Brexit ...

So does abandoning its neighbours do Great Britain any
favours?
Does it ease the tensions on the state?
Global pressures will be endless to the lonely and the
friendless
When our banks and companies migrate.

Brexit, oh Brexit ...

In a world of terrorist hate, security will dominate;
So is Britain better going it alone?
Or is there greater common sense in sharing the
intelligence
To deal with threats from sources yet unknown?

Brexit, oh Brexit ...

A mature nation would surely not throw its toys out of
the cot
When it doesn't agree with partner states?
Time to ditch the mental chains and exercise more
mature brains
To find solutions to which all relate.

Major Rager   Page 117

Prose and Cons – Poems Against The Brexit Machine

Brexit, oh Brexit ...

The European main endeavour to end Europe's wars for
ever
And to guarantee that hate and rancour cease.
The different nationalities don't all share practicalities
But the goal's the same: to guarantee the peace.

Brexit, oh Brexit ...

If immigration folds your brow, have you yet wondered
how
A country copes without young people's aid?
In a geriatric nation there'll be no consideration
Of who'll do the work to get our pensions paid.

Brexit, oh Brexit ...

For us to reach our full potential, creative thinking is
essential.
Prosperity depends on forward vision
Of mulling all perspectives through to come to a well-
reasoned view,
And making wise and rational decisions.

NL

Who's Winning Now?

This was not a game anyone could win.
So when you have say that we have lost, well that's
when the conflicts begin.
We need to unite to fight for what is right and true.
On this Earth we are equal, I am no better than you.

It's a thin disguise, I can see it in your eyes,
Burning with deceit and lies – hear my protesting cries.
Because I'm not afraid to fight for what I know to be
right
And for what I want to be true, I will stand up to you.

So the campaign is over, judgement has come and gone.
We've laid our weapons to rest, and you think that you
have won.
But where do you go from here? There never was a plan.
And when you got what you thought you wanted, you
turned away and ran.

So we're on this railroad, heading to an unknown fate.
We've spoken words in anger, discrimination and hate.
Our world is sick with violence, we don't need another
war;
When a stranger comes for help, how could you shut the
door?

This was not a game, but you've dealt me all your cards,
So when we reach our home-made hell, I'll send you my
kind regards.

Major Rager

Oh, when will this be over, when will this madness
cease?
We'll take our fair share of hardship, for the sake of
peace.

It's a thin disguise, we can see it in your eyes,
Burning with deceit and lies – hear our protesting cries.
Because we're not afraid to fight for what we know to be
right
And for what we want to be true, we will stand up to
you.

Madeleina Kay

The DUP-er

to the tune of 'The Irish Rover'

I've been a DUP-er for many's the year,
And I spent all me money on bombings and beer,
But now I'm colluding with UKIP CON DUP,
And we never will be terrorists no more!

And it's D, U, P never, May, DUP never no more
Will I join the Coalition, no, never no more.

I went into the Commons I used to frequent,
And I told Ma Theresa me money was spent.
I asked her for two billion, she answered me, 'Yay,
Such a coalition of chaos as you I can't have any day.'

And it's D, U, P, never ...

I took up from my pocket ten nuclear weapons,
And Theresa said she was in seventh heaven.
She said, 'I have Trident, and bombs of the best,
And the words that you told me were only in jest.'

And it's D, U, P, never ...

I'll go home to Theresa, confess that I'm a gay,
And I'll ask her to confirm that she wants me to stay.
And when I'm converted, as oft times before,
I never will be a GAY-DUP no more.

And it's D, U, P, never ...

Peter Cook

Christmas Corner

Scandal Bells

Jingle bells, Brexit's hell
For Theresa May:
Can't be fun to face another
Scandal every day.
Oh!

Jingle bells, Brexit's hell,
Won't she go away?
Once she's gone, I only hope
We'll see a brighter day.

'Taking back control';
Of what they didn't say.
Thanks to Russian trolls,
They still got their way.

Now Theresa's stuck
Pretending it's all fine,
Though she knows her party's fucked.
Let's hope they all resign.
Oh!

Jingle bells, Brexit's hell
For Theresa May:
Can't be fun to face another

Scandal every day.
Oh!

Jingle bells, Brexit's hell,
Won't she go away?
Once she's gone, I only hope
We'll see a brighter day.

Paul Brown

We Wish You a Merry Christmas

We wish you a merry Christmas,
We wish you a merry Christmas,
We wish you a merry Christmas
And a happy new year.

And we're not going to stand for Brexit,
We're not going to stand for Brexit,
We're not going to stand for Brexit,
Cos we want to stay IN.

We all want to travel freely,
We all want to travel freely,
We all want to travel freely
With our EHIC cards.

And we'll stay in the single market,
And we'll stay in the single market,
And we'll stay in the single market
Because it makes sense.

Major Rager

And Brexit is wrecking Britain,
And Brexit is wrecking Britain,
And Brexit is wrecking Britain,
So give up and STAY.

We wish you a merry Christmas ...

Evelyn Leslie

The Brexit Grinch Song

My daddy told me not to fear,

When the Brexit Grinch appeared this year:

'Don't you worry now, it'll all be fine.

We can eat our Christmas cake and drink our wine.'

Santa Claus, where did you go?

Santa Claus, I'm out here in the snow.

I've been waiting all night long,

And I'm starting to think there's something wrong!

You need a visa now if you come from a different nation,

But the Home Office has rejected Santa's application.

His work's inconsistent, he might become a burden on
the state,

He's made his appeal, Amber Rudd will decide his fate!

Rudolph is ready, rigged up to the sleigh,

He turns his nose light on and they're on their way.

But the border guards stop him with a sneer:

Turns out his EU pet passport isn't valid here!

Flying across the sky, high up in the night,
On a Christmas Eve, it's such a festive sight!
But flights are grounded over the UK,
So Santa has to go on foot with his loaded sleigh.

It's getting late, and Santa's still not come.
Looks like the Brexit Grinch has stolen all our fun.
Santa's been stopped again, for customs checks;
They're unwrapping all the presents, goodness knows
what's next!

We can't have our Christmas cake *and* eat it;
No, the Brexit Grinch must be defeated!
So tell that Brexit Grinch to go away –
He's not welcome here, no, he can't stay!
The only Christmas gift I really want to have
Is my EU citizenship and my passport back!

Madeleina Kay

Major Rager

The Twelve Days of Christmas (EU Style)

On the first day of Christmas, the EU gave to me: the
freedom to travel visa-free.
On the second day of Christmas, the EU gave to me: free
health insurance.
On the third day of Christmas, the EU gave to me:
Erasmus.
On the fourth day of Christmas, the EU gave to me: tariff-
free trade.
On the fifth day of Christmas, the EU gave to me: FORTY
YEARS OF PEACE.
On the sixth day of Christmas, the EU gave to me: all our
clean beaches.
On the seventh day of Christmas, the EU gave to me:
food-labelling.
On the eighth day of Christmas, the EU gave to me:
improved workers' rights.
On the ninth day of Christmas, the EU gave to me:
investment in regions.
On the tenth day of Christmas, the EU gave to me:
consumer protection.
On the eleventh day of Christmas, the EU gave to me:
free mobile roaming.
On the twelfth day of Christmas, the EU gave to me:
drugs regulations.

Evelyn Leslie

We Wish You a Happy Brexit

We wish you a happy Brexit,
We wish you a happy Brexit,
We wish you a happy Brexit,
But don't hold your breath.

Sad tidings we bring:
The bells never ring.
There won't be a happy Brexit:
We're screwed and that's that.

The WTO
Brings nothing but woe.
There won't be a happy Brexit:
There's no hope of that.

NL

Prose and Prose Poetry

Prose and Cons

I have never before witnessed the sheer numbers of people who have been moved to activism on a political issue over such an extended period. In this section we find a series of pieces of prose that exorcise the Brexit beast. Rather like the quest to defeat Lord Voldemort in *Harry Potter*, the Brexit beast cannot be defeated with a single blow. We must find all the Brexit horcruxes and destroy them one by one. This means legal challenges, petitions, marches, lobbying, music and so on. Yet the myths of Europe persist, due to brainwashing by our populist media. Here's a few of the myths debunked, from the article 'Should I Stay or Should I Go?' which I wrote just before the referendum. Although it gained 20,000 views on LinkedIn, I suspect it was not read by those who needed to see it.

'It costs each of us around 37 pence per day to belong to the EU club. That's less than the price of half a Mars Bar! So what do we get for this?

1. No major wars in seventy years

2. Free movement and relatively simple border controls when compared with other parts of the world

3. The ability to trade and work freely in Europe

4. Investment in large infrastructure and academic research projects that are otherwise hard to finance, e.g. the Sage Gateshead and the Millennium Bridge in London

5. Sovereignty – it is an enduring myth that we are getting our country back. We never lost it, and this was even confirmed in our shoddy Brexit bill by Parliament. We have managed to wage wars without reference to Europe, and the recent calls by Leave voters for Europe to interfere in Catalonia prove just how little information we have'

Of course, all political systems have their faults, yet many of the faults reported by Leave voters and politicians are in fact faults of our own parliamentary system in Westminster. Pointing fingers is easy and cheap. Here our authors expound some of the myths and facts about our Brexit past, present and futures.

Asbestos Roof

Once upon a time there was a huge house with lots of people living in it. One day someone in the house decided it would be a good idea to have a vote on whether to get rid of the old roof, because here and there, over the decades, a few tiles had slipped and occasionally they let in a bit of rain. They could replace it with a brand-new, lightweight, waterproof, fireproof one made of the finest asbestos. Not everyone voted, but 52 per cent of those who did voted to get rid of the slightly leaky roof and replace it with an asbestos one.

After that decision was made there was a feeling of elation and triumph among those who had long wanted, and were now delighted and excited to have the prospect of, change and a new roof.

However, before the new roof could be installed there appeared a highly disturbing report from reputable researchers, who had no connections with either the asbestos or the tiling industries, that asbestos was a substance so toxic and hazardous that it should never be used in house construction. Some of those who had pushed hardest for a new roof had been well aware of the risks of asbestos, but had kept quiet about it and pushed for it anyway, because, for reasons of their own, they had a visceral hatred for the old tiled roof.

So, a decision to get that nice, new asbestos roof had been made by a 4 per cent majority of those who had voted. Many of those who voted for the asbestos roof loudly and aggressively insisted that the change should go ahead, despite the fact that scientists had informed them that it was more or less guaranteed there would be sickness and fatalities, particularly among the most vulnerable: young people, old people, those with restricted mobility.

The more that people expressed concern about their survival under an asbestos roof, the new-roofers became ever more shrill and insistent that they absolutely must have the new roof because they had won the vote, fair and square. Some pointed out that concealing the truth about the dangers inherent in a new asbestos roof made the referendum very far from fair and square.

In light of the new information about the significant hazards of an asbestos roof, some individuals argued that since it would be tantamount to suicide to have an asbestos roof it would be wiser and safer for everyone who lived in the house to abandon altogether the radical decision to have a new roof, and instead put their energy and resources into funding and commissioning some good tilers to repair and replace the old tiles wherever necessary. Imagine that.

Sheree Burgess points out: It wasn't a complete vote anyway because there were a couple of people who normally lived in the house who were working abroad when the vote was taken and were not able to give their opinion in time.

Bridget Veldhuis adds: Likewise several people who had been invited to live in the house (paying rent of course), and staying for often quite a long time, were told they were not allowed to have a say. And then they were told they were only guests and it was time they thought about leaving.

Rajan Naidu

Drain the Swamp

In Aldous Huxley's dystopian *Brave New World*, written in 1932, the people are controlled through the distribution of daily doses of addictive 'soma' tablets. Today's governments have access to far more sophisticated methods to manage gullible electorates. The trick is to convince a majority of people, through 'friendly' media, that they live in a 'special' country, superior to others and not answerable to normal rules of international diplomacy. In that way, problems can always be pinned on external factors that threaten the fantasy world so created.

This was a tactic employed by Hitler and Stalin in the 1930s and 40s; and since then, the modern candidates for state-empowered reality manipulation are many and various: Putin, Kim Jong-un, the Chinese government, Erdogan etc. 'Strong leadership' means that the people no longer need to think for themselves, simply to rationalise the messages presented to them by government and their channels of communication.

Education becomes a tool of government, its sole purpose to guide young people through examinations that require only the skill of memory and not those of reasoning, questioning, evidence-gathering, critical judgement, nor the development of vision, empathy and understanding.

This is what is now beginning to happen in the UK and America. Create a sense of national paranoia: the 'others', including our neighbours and colleagues in other nations, are milking us, are out to get us. They threaten our way of life. So we need strong leaders to make our countries great again – because our countries are special.

Drain the swamp of everyone who disagrees or has a different culture. Reduce education to the basics and starve it of funds. And the tabloid press oblige by publishing the messages as self-evident truths. It is the equivalent of Huxley's soma tablets. Blind, brainless, flag-waving so-called patriots with little critical judgement or understanding of economic consequence, international protocols or global cultures are empowered as foot soldiers to implement the strategy.

And the world moves into reverse again. The UK is well on the way to destroying its heritage of tolerant open-mindedness. Thanks to the soma of the compliant media, the poison has been assimilated into the British psyche and the future becomes the uncertain hostage to the winds of intolerance, bigotry and manipulation.

Another recent development takes us back to Huxley's dark vision. In his predicted future world, live childbirth is banned. Women are liberated from the pain and inconvenience of rearing children; instead babies are factory-generated in artificial birthing chambers. They are even sorted into five categories of work type named alpha, beta, gamma, delta and epsilon, dependent on the work they would do for the 'good of society'. Alphas, the few, would be the genetically selected leaders; epsilons would do the menial tasks within a strictly regulated social system, kept quiescent by soma. The first step towards this world was announced in June 2017, with the revelation that artificial birthing pods had been successfully tested in the USA, using embryos taken from women.

Oh brave new world, that this should become humanity's dismal fate.

NL

The Big Debate

Are there any foreign companies in Britain?

Yep! Hundreds of them. They range from biggies like Microsoft and Nissan to smaller research and media ones.

So how many jobs do they provide?

Well at the last count it was between two and four million Brits.

So many? Why are these companies here?

Well, it's mostly because Britain's in Europe – that's a marketplace potential of 600 million people in twenty-seven countries.

So if Britain came out of the EU, would they stay?

Are you kidding? They'd be off like that stuff off a shovel.

What about the jobs?

Yep, them too.

How about the banks – isn't the financial services industry Britain's biggest money spinner?

Yep, and there's a lot of 'em in the City.

So would they go too?

I think you could work that out for yourself. The welcoming arms of Frankfurt, Dublin, Paris and Amsterdam come to mind. And the exodus has already started.

Hey, that's a lot of lost jobs – so what happens to the British economy then?

Down the pan, of course.

But the empire will strike back, won't it? You know: Australia, New Zealand, Canada?

You are joking, aren't you? The empire hasn't existed for more than eighty years.

We should never have got rid of it in the first place.

I think you'll find that they got rid of us – they wanted their independence.

But we're Brits – we're special. The world owes us.

Tell that to the fairies at the bottom of your garden.

So what does that mean for those of us who are left?

Doesn't bear thinking about, does it? That's a lot of soup kitchens.

Major Rager

Well at least those bloody foreigners won't be coming to pinch our jobs.

That's probably because there won't be any to pinch.

Why did we allow so many in anyway?

I suppose it was to do the jobs we couldn't or wouldn't do. Oh, and they give us a different perspective on things – widen our horizons, so to speak.

I don't want my horizons widening.

That's pretty obvious – but the economy needs people who do.

Why?

Could be because the world's changing very fast and our country has to keep up with it. Creative people with vision are scarce.

So what's Europe got to do with that?

Well, for instance, we can't afford to pay for all the research that makes us prosperous ourselves, so we have to do it jointly with our neighbours. The environment, climate change, pollution don't respect borders, and neither does organised crime. Then there's the fact that our global competitors are much bigger. Europe together carries a lot more clout than a very small island off its north-west coast. Oh, and Europe already provides 40 per cent of our wealth in trade.

Yeah, but it takes billions from us.

Well, nothing comes for free. On balance we gain much more than we lose. And the young people love it because they can live in a wider world with a wider culture-set.

Why would they want to do that? It's not natural.

What do you mean, it's not natural?

Well they'd lose all their mates and family an 'all.

I guess that opening their minds to new experiences takes preference. Sounds more exciting to me too. Wish I were younger. I'd be off like a dog with diarrhoea.

Not me. Them foreigners give me the creeps. They're not like us.

Oh, you mean the two-headed ones and that race with the three legs and only one arm?

Don't be silly. You know what I mean. They speak different and they're trying to bully us into submission.

Where did you get that idea?

It was in the *Daily Mail*. They're always finding things out like that. They won't negotiate on our terms.

That's maybe because we aren't being very intelligent and we are trying to bully them. After all, it was us who wanted to leave. We can expect a rough time in the future.

How's that?

Well, all the things we were talking about earlier – jobs, economy, no investment, companies leaving.

Oh, that. It's worth it to have control of our borders.

But we already have control of our borders.

How do you make that out? That funny fellow with the mop said in the *Sun* that we finally have our borders back.

I know who you mean. But what happens when an aeroplane lands? Doesn't everybody queue up to show their passports? Seaports too, except that the passport is examined on the other side. That's done by our border force. We never lost our borders.

Well, he said something about sovereignty too. That's important.

What do you mean by sovereignty?

I don't know, but if he says it, it must be important. I'm not racist or anything like that. But them immigrants – they're all lazy and they only come here for the benefits.

Who told you that?

That nice Mr Farage. At least he's got it right!

No comment …

NL

The Great British Cake Scoff (Florentine Recipe)

Ingredients:
50g buttering up
50g plainly floored
50g sugar (for the pill)
50g totally nuts
200g very dark shock-a-lot
Very little candid appeal
Finely chopped cherry-picking

Method:
Mix up together.
Cause a stir.
Dollop on to well prepared broadsheet.
Bake until browned off.
Smother in very dark shock-a-lot.
Have cake. Eat it.

Jane Berry

On Patriotism

In these difficult Brexit days, those who oppose the suicidal self-harm that Britain is proposing to implement are often accused of 'lacking patriotism'. But that depends on what we believe patriotism means.

There is a patriotism that kills. It pulls down the blinds, mean-minded, frightened, self-focused, brain-dead, xenophobic, with the vision of a dead mole – insular. It leads to conflict, resentment, anger and eventually to war, the UKIP/Britain First/Trump persuasion within every country. It's easily exploited by press, politicians and would-be dictators.

There's another kind of patriotism – it's open-minded, tolerant and understanding. It recognises diversity, exchanges ideas, concepts and experiences with other people and nations, understands the source of prosperity and compassion. It doesn't close down, it opens up minds, brains and hearts to the realities of a twenty-first-century global world, threatened by climate change, human greed and rampant ignorance. It seeks to find ways of righting its wrongs that will preserve that prosperity, address disadvantage and allow nations and people to live together in peace. Because it's a thinking patriotism, it's less susceptible to manipulation.

That's my kind of patriotism – not the dead-end of blind, self-serving groups of mean-spirited so-called patriots, the single-minded UKIP lookalikes that are endemic in Britain, France, the USA and every country that has the arrogance to believe itself to be special and brainwashes its people to believe it.
NL

Prose and Cons – Poems Against The Brexit Machine

A Humble Suggestion

It won't happen, I know, but maybe this is a rational approach to the present impasse.

1. The government should confess that it has no clue what outcome the Brexit talks should aim for, nor what a majority of the country thinks now (as opposed to what they were persuaded to think a year ago). Real democracy recognises that people can change their mind, and gives them the right to do so.

2. It should appoint a panel of those people whose sectors will be most affected – industrialists, economists, hospital managers, educators, financiers etc. – and ask them to produce a report on the likely consequences of Brexit for each sector. It should include ordinary people from civil society.

3. The panel should be given three months to do so. And to list the indicators by which they have come to their conclusions.

4. No leakages to the press or to politicians. The report should be published and publicised to the whole nation.

5. There should then be a second referendum, this time with the pros and cons of Brexit set out clearly and posted to every household.

6. The voters in that referendum should be ALL those who are affected by Brexit, including expats now

Major Rager

disenfranchised, EU people who have lived in UK for more than three years, and all people in the UK age over sixteen. (Personally I would give people below thirty two votes, since they are the ones who have to live longer with the consequences. But that's perhaps too rational.)

7. The money spent on this should strictly monitored – no donations from home-based or foreign millionaires – and press comment should be monitored for veracity and fairness.

8. The results should be relayed to the Brexit negotiators and the appropriate action taken.

This reasoned approach would be more indicative of the seriousness of the decision-making process, treating people as active learners rather than passive accepters of clever propaganda. Moreover, this would be true democracy, where people are allowed to change their minds based on emerging intelligence and likely consequence. For those reasons this proposal stands no chance whatsoever.

NL

Who Are the Patriots?

The British media and Brexiters often accuse those who chose to remain in the European Union as lacking in patriotism. But who are the true British patriots? Are they ...

Those who uphold the traditional British values of openness, tolerance and fair play, or
those xenophobes who want to close borders to foreigners and send them home?

Those who think things through and work out the consequences for Britain before they make a big decision, or
those who allow their opinions to be decided by absentee press owners and/or politicians on the make?

Those who wish the British economy to remain prosperous and dynamic, or
those who take huge risks with the economy's future prosperity?

Those who encourage the maintenance of British jobs through inward investment and the growth of British companies, or
those who by their actions threaten continued investment and employment in Britain?

Those who recognise that prosperity depends on immigration, or
those who are deliberately blind to the benefits of

immigration?

Those who cherish the meaning of a United Kingdom, or
those who create the conditions for its break-up?

Those who want to open up opportunities for young
people in Europe, or
those who want to close down the opportunities for
young people in Europe?

Those who believe in the rule of law, or
those who want to bypass the rule of law for political
gain?

Those with open minds who believe in diversity and
international friendships, or
those with closed minds who shout the odds about
patriotism, nationalism and racism?

Those who work out what's best for Britain before
making a decision, or
those who act out of a false, brainless patriotism
whether or not it's good for Britain?

Those who prepare for negotiation by remaining calm
and non-confrontational, or
those who prepare for negotiation by slagging off their
fellow negotiators before they even start?

Those with vision who offer hope for the future, or
those who offer only hate xenophobia and bigotry in the
present?

Major Rager

So who are the real patriots? You tell me.

NL

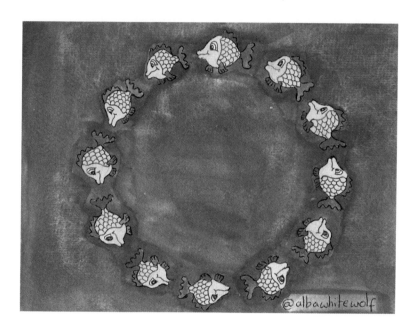

Typology of a Brexiteer

Brexiteers tend to fit into one or more of the following categories:

The Empire Loyalist: Lives under the delusion that Britain still has an empire and, if it hasn't, it jolly well should have so that we can show the buggers what's what!

The **Brainless Patriot**: Lives under the delusion that Britain is best at everything, and if it isn't it's always the Johnny Foreigners' fault. Often disappointed at soccer tournaments, believes expats are traitors.

The **Easily Led Tabloid Reader**: Lives under the delusion that the *Sun*, *Mail*, *Telegraph* and *Express* tell the truth, and they are not, repeat not, being led by the nose by absentee billionaires with their own agenda.

The **Trusting Follower**: Lives under the delusion that Nigel, Michael and Boris (and Arron) are honourable people who don't tell fibs in order to advance their political prospects.

The **Poor Family Man**: Who isn't getting a good deal and will oppose the bastards who put him and his family there, even if it means ruining the country's economy.

The **Starry-eyed Optimist**: Who lives under the Panglossian delusion that all is for the best in this best of all possible worlds ... and has thinking skills to match.

The **Grumpy Pensioner**: Who can't keep up with change in modern life and still lives under the delusion that Britain can stay exactly as they think it ought to be, and didn't we win the bloody war?

The **Britain First Bovver Boy**: The equivalent of Hitler's brownshirts and Mosley's blackshirts, who makes sure that the Krauts, Wogs, Dagos, Polaks and Frogs will be ejected from the country as soon as he gets the word from Nutto.

The **Dithery Politician**: Who lives under the delusion that voting for Brexit against his/her beliefs and instincts is reasonable behaviour.

The **Rat-brained Rationaliser**: Whose connection with reasoning, evidence- gathering and critical thinking is at best delusional, but knows what he thinks and has no need for experts to tell him otherwise.

The word 'delusion' somehow keeps cropping up. Wonder why?

NL

Back to Tribalism

There appears to be a tabloid-fuelled fantasy mind-world

where Britain is somehow special because it's Britain

where its economy will magically continue to be strong by ditching half its trading partners

where employment will mystically continue to increase by discouraging those global investors who use Britain as a conduit to the European marketplace

where xenophobia reigns so that anything that is 'not British' is corrupt (as if Britain were a shining example of fairness)

where insularity is a desirable virtue

where the country is miraculously more secure by isolating itself from its neighbours.

In this jingoistic, paranoid world Britain is the fount of wisdom, knowledge and goodness and there is nothing to learn from our European colleagues. They become Krauts, Frogs, Wops, Dagos and any other derogatory word used to describe 'not British'.

They're out to steal our money, take our jobs, dilute our culture and ruin our economy. Not a word about how incomers provide new insights into other cultures, how they are a net asset to the economy, pay taxes and provide new opportunities for job and infrastructure creation.

Nor how European trade creates employment and income for hundreds of British companies, boosts living standards, encourages companies from Japan, USA, Australia, Europe and other parts of the world to establish their headquarters in Battleship Britain in order to access the half-a-billion European marketplace.

It took an American president to articulate what is obvious to every thinking person with the future of their country at heart. The real nature of this fast-changing, multi-faceted world. The apoplectic response to his observations demonstrates the poverty of vision and reason in the Brexit camp. Not once was the verity of his thesis questioned – only the temerity of a foreigner in expressing it.

Get real, people! Blind patriotism is fine on the football field, but in the harsh twenty-first-century world of international business, politics, Trump and terrorism, small countries need partners in order to stand up to massive global corporations and trading conglomerates.

The people need to look outwards with confidence, not inwards with resentment. And they need to be pragmatic and open-minded. The empire, and the superiority mind-set it fostered, is long dead.

The EU may not be perfect – what large organisation of nations is? – but it has brought sixty years of peace and prosperity into a continent noted mainly for a thousand years of squabbling and war. Do we really want to go backwards into a tribal 'my country's better than yours' nightmare à la Trump, where ideals are dead, pragmatism is irrelevant and xenophobia controls minds and actions?

UKIP and the Brexiteers would have it so, and so it seems would the absentee owners of the tabloid press and the political chancers with personal ambition and/or blinkered mind-sets.

Britain does have much to offer, not only to Europe but to the world as a whole. But it also has much to learn from them. Once any country or any person stops learning they might as well be dead.

NL

Two-storey Building

1. You're playing a game with another team.

The other team has made you rich through trading with them

Because that's the way that world trade works today.

Other countries buy tickets for the game because you are in the game.

That provides a lot of jobs for your country.

But there are some things you don't like about the way the other team plays.

So do you sulk, join Brexit, pick up your ball and go home?

Some politicians see it as a chance to advance their career and the press supports them.

Is that the way an intelligent country should behave?

Or is that the way of wimps and losers?

Or –can you think it through, use your head, continue to play and work out the differences between you?

Now that's the intelligent way. Win-win. It's up to you.
2.

2. There's a difference between reasoning and rationalising.

Reasoning means looking at the evidence over all the issues and making a decision based on fact.

If there is little fact, probability theory often helps to create probable fact.

Rationalising means twisting facts to fit what you want to think

Or what clever manipulators persuade you to want to think.

They use half-truths, avoid-truths, myths, fear of change and often downright lies.

There's a lot of that going on in the Brexit debate and people are buying it.

Probable fact tells us that the British economy will suffer greatly, that jobs will disappear and that companies will go bust.

In Brexit-speak, that's scaremongering, i.e. a Brexit avoid-truth.

A true patriot reasons it out, sees through the crap and doesn't gamble with the country's future – that's not a fact but it's an intelligent action based on fact.

NL

Ready for Take-off

Pilot: Ready for take-off.

Steward: But there aren't any wings on the plane, sir.

Pilot: Listen, you cretin, we had a referendum and we won. Ready for take-off.

Steward: With respect, sir. The plane can't take off without wings.

Pilot: Who says that then?

Steward: Well, sir, the aeronautical engineers, designers and other experts.

Pilot: We won. We don't need experts. Ready for take-off.

Steward: But sir, if you try to take off, you'll just run off the end of the runway and all the passengers will perish.

Pilot: Listen, we won. That's Project Fear. You lost. Get used to it.

Steward: But, sir, for the sake of the passengers, won't you see reason?

Pilot. Reason? I'll tell you what's reason. They voted for it too. That's reason. Now we won, you lost, let's get on with it.

Major Rager

Steward: Right, sir. I hope you don't mind but I'm out of here. Off to France.

Pilot: You're a traitor to your country, steward! Engines to the ready. Here we go. We won, we won. We won.

CRASH!!!!!!!!!!!

Faint voice off: We won, we won, we won, get over it.

NL

About the Authors

NL is a former professor of lifelong learning who has never stopped learning. He has been a labourer on a building site; a teacher of statistics and geography; a project manager with a territory of Europe, the Middle East and Africa; a world traveller; a self-employed worker, a writer and poet. Proud to be British, European and a world citizen of everywhere and not nowhere, he is sad that his beautiful, tolerant country has been taken over by rich charlatans, newspaper owners and politicians with the means to con so many of his countrymen into national suicide.

Peter Cook leads Human Dynamics and The Academy of Rock, offering organisation development and masterclasses on business. He is author of and contributor to twelve books on leadership. His three passions are science, business and music, having led innovation teams for eighteen years to develop life-saving drugs, including human insulin and the first treatments for HIV/AIDS. He has been playing music since the age of four, led the musical direction of No. 10 Vigil from its inception, and formed Rage Against the Brexit Machine to reach into people's visceral system via the arts. His mission is to Break Brexit Before Brexit Breaks Britain.

Madeleina Kay, a.k.a. EU Supergirl, is an artist, singer and writer who is fighting Brexit with fun, not fear.

Vicki Harris is a freelance book editor and proof reader, fighting Brexit for her children's sake. She lives in Barnet, north London, but belongs in East Anglia and France.

Peter Roberts is a teacher, youth worker and tutor. He lives in Buckinghamshire. His hobbies include cycling, mountaineering, bird-watching and plaguing Jacob Rees-Mogg. His sole complaint about our fellow Europeans is that some Belgians run his beloved football club, Charlton Athletic, and do it badly. His children fortunately have dual UK and EU citizenship, but he fights for those who are not so lucky.

Jane Berry is an award-winning innovator in international development for health in developing countries. A multilingual, multicultural citizen of the world, she has lived and worked in South America and the Caribbean, southern and north Africa, and Europe.

Peter St John is a London-born chartered engineer, now retired. He writes novels from his home in France. http://www.peterstjohn.net/index_56.htm

Lesley Bell is a member of the No. 10 Vigil and a founder member of Rage Against the Brexit Machine. She performs songs as herself and as alter ego Granny Remain. She is also a teacher, wife, mother and grandmother who wants her country back.

Gemma Knowles is a British migrant mother of three, living in Germany.

Helen Cooney is a generation X-er living in Bristol whose interests include theatre, functional medicine and epigenetics, Italian language and culture, and art history.

Marc Perry lives in west Wales. He works as a care assistant at a local nursing home and is a part-time poet and author.

Paul Brown, from Glasgow, speaks fluent German, tourist French, pub Dutch and restaurant Italian. Married to a

German-speaking Belgian, he is to his knowledge the only person ever to submit an honours dissertation on the German sense of humour.

Rajan Naidu is a person whose interests include good community; peace; justice; human rights; protecting our environment; good ideas and their communication and implementation; encouraging political and social engagement; unity; concerted, intelligent action; speaking truth to power . . . that sort of thing.

Annie Bell is a member of the No. 10 Vigil and Rage Against the Brexit Machine. An aspiring writer, self-confessed Europhile, proud European and speaker of four European languages, she is absolutely convinced that remaining in the EU is the only sensible option for Britain.

Robert Cunliffe is a modern-languages graduate, poet, guitar teacher and person-centred counsellor. He has spent years living abroad, mostly in France, but currently lives in Liverpool.

Printed in Great Britain
by Amazon